Shadows Of Light

By

Eric S. Hintz

First published by AuthorHouse 06/16/04

ISBN: 1-4184-7586-6 (e-book)
ISBN: 1-4184-2706-3 (Paperback)

Printed in the United States of America
Bloomington, IN

This book is printed on acid free paper.

This is for my wife and kids

For my mothers and fathers

&

For all of the others

You know who you are

Thank you for your unconventional wisdom

__Preface__

Welcome to my book. I would first like to say that this short book was a pleasure to write, and that it is with great joy that I share it with you. This small story has been my pride and joy, as well as a source of migraines and frustration for the past year and a half. You see, this novella is more than just a story; it is something that happened to me. It happened to me one night after putting the children in bed and turning down the lights. It happened in the blink of an eye, and there was no turning back. There it was, *Shadows Of Light,* the title, characters, plot, story, the vision. It happened so fast that I didn't even realize that I was walking towards the computer rather than my bed. Before I knew it I had a dozen or so pages and was swimming in delight over what I had written. It wasn't much really, but I couldn't see that. I only saw what it was to become, and enjoyed every step in the process of trying to mold my idea into tangible form. I finished the story in less than two weeks.

I felt great, especially for a writer who had been struggling with several rewrites of my first novel, *Biland Shadows,* an epic fantasy that was taking me years to complete. Though soon after finishing this story I completed *Biland Shadows* as well, which is when all of my anguish began.

As for most aspiring writers out there, you already know how tedious and tormenting the publishing process can be for a new writer, for the rest of you, I suppose that you will have to take my word for it. Anyway, I had decided to publish my first book myself, if for no other reason than to see my work in print while avoiding the chaos of the publishing industry. But, which book to publish? The epic full-length fantasy, which I had spent years developing? Or this forty thousand-word wonder that I could not get out of my mind? Or even one of my many other projects that were near completion?

It is plainly obvious which book I chose, but not the reason why. I have always considered myself to be insightful and intuitive as well as charismatic in my creative endeavors. Developing this story was pure joy, and I cannot help but believe that the ecstasy a writer feels while writing a story spills over into the language, and is ultimately received and shared by the readers. Besides, this is one tale that would not let go of me until I had seen it through to completion.

It is my utmost hope that you have as much fun reading this story, as it was my pleasure to write. With all of this being said, please enjoy.

DELVID FROST

The earth's tired eyes close, as night does take
its place.
A silhouette of light from a dying sun shines
cold upon its face
Flowers hide with closed petals, and fall with
broken stems.
As death is called from mountaintops.

RUBY MEADOWS

SHADOWS OF LIGHT

1

Ruby meadows grimaced as she gently rubbed her swollen knuckles. Her arthritis was flaring up again and she knew through experience that a storm was brewing. Her arthritis always acted up when the weather grew severe. She could sense the changing weather patters with the increase and decrease of her arthritic pains, which were often more reliable than the schooled meteorologists on the television. She could feel the approach and passing of warm and cold fronts alike, as well as anticipating the rising and falling of the temperature. Today her sore old bones were telling her that a thunderstorm was imminent, and as her aches worsened she knew that is was going to be a nasty one. Usually her old bones and joints gave her little trouble, though on days like these, when the weather turned sour, it made it difficult to do even the simplest of tasks, such as preparing dinner as she was doing now.

Ruby sighed as she tried to ignore her discomfort, and then decided to take one of the painkillers that her physician had prescribed. After taking her oxycontin tablet she checked the roast that had been in the oven, and turned off the broccoli that she had been steaming on the stove. Looking for her husband she walked out of the kitchen and into the living room. The television was on, but she saw no sign of Clifford.

"Dinner is almost ready Cliff," she hollered to him, guessing that he was in the bathroom.

"I am right here!" said Cliff as he lay on the sofa. He stretched as if he had been asleep and then sat up to face his wife. She had a surprised look on her face and he smiled.

"Sorry," she said as she smiled back. "I did not see you there. Dinner is almost ready," she said again quietly.

"It smells great," he remarked as he stood up.

An ear splitting clap of thunder resounded and they looked to each other for comfort as the thin walls of their doublewide trailer trembled under the low rumbling that was left in its wake. Together they walked over the large picture window and peered out into the gloomy afternoon sky. The cloud-filtered daylight had an odd hazel color that made the day look otherworldly and ethereal. The thick thunderheads moved rapidly above them hastily heading towards the north.

"It looks like it is going to be a bad one," said Cliff as he took his wife's hand and looked into her eyes. He loved her dearly. More now than on the day they were married some fifty-four years ago. Her hazel eyes reflected the strange light outside, and the deep wrinkles on her face somehow made her even more beautiful, perhaps because he had watched them grow over the years and was more familiar with hers than his own. He brushed her long white hair out of her eyes and away from her face, and kissed her softly on the forehead. She was seventy-nine years old, three years younger than him. They were as healthy as one might expect. Cliff had bouts with his angina and troublesome prostate, while Ruby was a breast cancer survivor and seemingly as strong as ever.

"I hate these storms," she said as she let go of his hand to give him a close hug, though not before petting him playfully on his pale bald head.

"I know you do," said Cliff as he hugged her back. "Is your arthritis acting up again?"

She nodded as her head rested upon his chest, and then looked up to the ominous sky as the soft pitter-patter of raindrops were heard on the rooftop. The wind began to howl fiercely and the sky grew dark as the storm front came upon them.

"Here it comes," said Cliff with a smile as the light trickle of rain instantly turned into a downpour so consuming that they could barely see the neighbors trailer home across the street. The sound of the rain was deafening as it pounded against the roof, and they had to raise their voices to hear each other over its persistent drumming.

"Wow," Ruby said with amazement as she hugged Cliff tightly.

"Would you look at that," Cliff said in wonder. "We haven't had a storm like this in years. Isn't it great?"

"You have always loved a good storm, haven't you?" Asked Ruby as she looked into her husband's eyes and smiled.

He nodded. "You have to admit that it is pretty amazing, isn't it. This is god's handy work at its best."

Ruby shook her head. "You can call it amazing, you can call it exciting, you can call it anything you like, but I call it scary."

"We will be fine," he assured her.

"You always say that," she muttered.

"And I have always been right, haven't I?"

Ruby let go of her husband with a kiss and a sigh. "Yeah, but one of these days your luck is going to run out, and silly me is going to be standing right there next to you." With that she kissed her husband again on the cheek as she went to tend to her roast.

"Yeah, yeah," Cliff replied as he followed her away from the window and into the kitchen.

A flash of lightning briefly illuminated the dreary day outside and was followed by another clap of thunder, though not nearly as loud as first. A few moments later the downpour receded into a steady rain that fell swiftly, but was however not as hard on they're hearing. The delicious aroma of the cooking pot roast filled the kitchen and their thoughts shifted to things other than the storm that was raging outside.

Cliff retrieved an almost full bottle of white zinfandel wine from the pantry, and two tall glasses from the cabinet. "How much longer until it is done?" He asked.

"Oh, about ten to twenty minutes or so," she said as she brought out two plates and began to set the table. She was tired today. The storm kept her edgy, as they usually did, but over all she was just plain exhausted. Aside from her stiffening arthritis, it was Sunday, and Sundays always made her tired, as the usual ritual of church and grocery shopping seemed to sap the strength from her old bones these days. They both enjoyed their Sundays out and would often stop to have lunch at a restaurant, or take a walk by the lake. They had few friends and did not get out much anymore. Nor had they any children or grandchildren to keep in touch with. They had a son once, long ago, but the pregnancy had been difficult and left her infertile. Their son was born healthy, and up until the age of five remained so. Although in his fifth year of life, their son Robert J. Meadows contracted a rare form of leukemia and died the day after his sixth birthday. This was a difficult time for them, as it was the anniversary of his birth and death, and if he had not died he would have turned fifty yesterday.

Ruby finished setting the dinner table and accepted the glass of wine that Cliff offered to her. He then poured a glass for himself and raised it to offer a toast.

Cliff smiled shyly as Ruby raised her glass to meet his. "To good storms and good company," he pronounced.

"And to those who could not be here with us today," Ruby added before their glasses met.

"Of course," Cliff acknowledged before sipping the wine.

Their attention jumped to the television as they heard the loud monotone buzzer of the emergency broadcast system, only this time it sounded different, more urgent as they heard the broadcast announcer repeat, "This is not a test."

The lightning bolt arced out of the heavy churning clouds and shot towards the earth. It blazed a brilliant path of blinding white light that struck outside of the trailer no more than twenty feet from where Cliff and Ruby stood. Ruby screamed as the blinding flash of the lightning caused her to lose her vision momentarily, and then screamed again as the ensuing thunder shook the foundation of their home causing pictures to fall of walls with breaking glass. Terrified she dropped her glass of wine, which shattered as it caught the edge of the table. With her heart pounding and her head spinning she reached for Cliff.

Cliff did not scream, but jumped when the thunder struck, and jumped again when Ruby reached for him. He quickly took her into his arms and found her trembling and shaken. His eyesight returned quickly though not without the splotches of color where the lightning had imprinted itself on his eyes. He found the trailer dark and without electricity.

"Oh great!" He said sarcastically, as he tried to calm Ruby as well as his racing heart. "It is okay honey. We are all right. It is just the storm, it is outside, and we are in here." He embraced her, resting her head on his shoulder. "It is okay baby." He said with a kiss.

Ruby was near tears and could feel her hands shaking as she and Cliff held each other. She felt a bit dizzy as her head began to clear from the adrenalin that was ebbing from her system, and she leaned on him for support.

"Jeepers!" she said somewhat out of breath. "I must be healthier than I thought."

"Why do you say that?" he inquired.

"Because I would have never in a million years believed that my heart could take a jolt like that."

They both laughed at themselves and in a few moments they began to calm down. She let go of her tight grip on him, and after assuring Cliff that she was all right they walked back to the window for another look at the storm. The power had gone out for the entire street, or for at least as much of it as they could see. The sky had now changed to a strange auburn color that was as intriguing as it was unsettling, and it seemed to be getting darker by the minute. It was still early, only three thirty, but one couldn't tell that by looking at the sky, which had the distinct appearance of dusk.

"Just what do you think you are doing?" asked Ruby as Cliff left her side and began fumbling around in the closet. He did not answer her right away and she waited patiently for his response, though she frowned when she saw him bring out an umbrella and his old raincoat.

"I am going to go outside and make sure that the lightning didn't start any fires," he said with determination as he began to slip his feet into a pair of shoes.

"You must be kidding me," she overstated dramatically. "You are going to get yourself killed! You are not supposed to go outside when there is lightning like that out there!"

"Don't you worry now," he said as he finished buttoning his coat, picked up the umbrella, and headed for the door.

Ruby shook her head, but did not attempt to talk him out of it. When Cliff made up his mind about something it usually stayed that way, and she knew how much he loved a good storm.

She remembered how when he was a younger man he would always dare to brave the storm. When the snow was too deep, or the flooding was too heavy, he would often drive for a while to survey the damage, help anyone in need, and enjoy the unique wonder that the storm stirred in him. As she watched him leave the house and enter into the rain she imagined that he was young again, enjoying the storm in the ways that he used to. She smiled when a strong gust of wind turned the umbrella inside out, and she laughed when the wind blew it out of his hands. Surprised, he tried to catch up with it unsuccessfully, and finally let it go. He then took a quick look around as the rain began to downpour once more. And she laughed again when he ran for the door as fast as his eighty-two year old legs would allow.

She tried to keep a straight face as she opened the door for him and waited. He scrambled through the entrance way soaked from head to toe. She could not hold it any longer and burst out into a fit of laughter.

"Where is your umbrella Mr. Fireman?" she chided.

Cliff was cold, wet, and not at all pleased. He was about to say so when he noticed how hard his wife was laughing. He had not seen her laugh like this in quite some time and did not want to spoil her fun. He imagined that he was probably an amusing sight, out there in the rain running after his umbrella. He grinned with a touch of embarrassment, as he too laughed harder than he had in a long while.

"My umbrella? Cliff asked. "Well, the neighbors are using it for a lawn ornament."

They continued to laugh as Ruby helped him out of his wet clothes. He then went to the bedroom to change into his pajamas while Ruby lit some candles and picked up the broken wine glass, still chuckling.

Feeling dry and somewhat refreshed, Cliff walked out of the bedroom and into the kitchen. He found his wife serving dinner on what looked to be a very romantic setting. The lights were off, the bottle of wine was out, with one glass replaced, and the flowers that she had picked yesterday still sat in full bloom in a vase on the table. The candlelight was the finishing touch that completed the atmosphere, and when he saw his wife bending over in the shadows he felt a stirring in his groin that he had not felt in over a year, at least a stirring that had not been Viagra induced. He went to her and took the dishes out of her hands and set them aside.

"What?" Ruby asked, although as she looked into his eyes she saw a spark that she had not seen in longer than she could remember. Forgetting about their early dinner they embraced kissing deeply, and as she held him closer she felt the extent of the spark that was rapidly growing into an unquenchable fire.

"Oh cliff," she said passionately. "We need storms like this more often."

Deciding to forego their dinner plans they retired to the bedroom. The passion was intense and unbridled as forgotten sensations and primal pleasures brought them together as one. Neither of them spoke as their limbs gripped each others wrinkled flesh with excitement. Time seemed to hold no meaning in this moment, and they were neither young nor old, but were lost in the delight of the love that they shared.

After their boundless passion lasted not once but twice, and as Ruby lay on her side holding her lover she felt a pang of discomfort in her chest. She shifted her weight as she tried to get comfortable, yet had little success and reluctantly decided to get out of bed.

"Where are you going?" Cliff asked with a disappointed expression and queer smile.

Ruby tried to hide her discomfort as she leaned down and kissed Cliff on the cheek. "I was just going to put that pot roast away before it goes bad. I will be back in a minute dear."

Cliff quickly kissed her on the lips and sat up with an elated smile. "Don't bother putting it away honey. I have actually worked up quite an appetite."

"Come on then, I will fix you a plate."

"You aren't going to eat?" He asked.

She shook her head. "No, not right now, maybe in a while. I think that this storm has got me on edge a bit, and then there is you, well let's just say that there hasn't been a hit like that since the Dodgers won the world series."

She said all of this with a smile as she avoided his eyes, and when she could avoid them no longer she found herself fighting back tears as she stood alone facing the specter of death that loomed in the back of her mind. There was a sense of impending doom that consumed her thoughts, heart, and soul, and she knew that the pain in her chest was not indigestion or anything else just as innocent.

She slipped on her purple robe that was complete with frills and ruffles, and then lit a candle.

"I love you," Cliff said as he lay there watching her.

"I love you too," she replied, and at that moment she almost forgot about the weight that she felt over her heart, though was reminded by a numb sensation in her left arm. She quickly left the room before the tears could come, before she could think too much about Cliff, and his possible reactions to her dying. A solitary tear leaked out of her eye as she thought about the errant productions of fate as they swirled in around her waiting for a chance to steal her last breath.

She went into the bathroom and closed the door behind her. Avoiding her reflection in the mirror she slid open the medicine cabinet that was concealed behind it. Unsure what exactly it was that she was looking for she rifled through the score of medicines until she found a bottle of asprin, although she doubled over in pain before she could take any. It felt to her as if someone had reached into her chest and had forcefully squeezed her heart. First she gripped her chest, and after the pain began to subside a bit she pounded on her left arm in an attempt to regain some of the feeling in it. Using her right hand she turned on the water faucet and quickly swallowed ten pills of asprin, five more doses than was recommended. She then retrieved a bottle of nitroglycerine tablets that Cliff kept on hand for his angina attacks that occurred occasionally. She placed five of them under her tongue along with another asprin just in case it might help.

As she closed the medicine cabinet Ruby peered into the mirror and suddenly felt as old as she looked. Her tired eyes were puffy and red, and her aged skin looked so pale in the candlelight that she decided that she already appeared dead. She splashed some cold water onto her face and she noticed that her severe pain was slowly diminishing. As she turned the water off she could once again hear the storm raging outside, and her thoughts turned back to Cliff. She wondered if she should mention this to him right now, right after what might have been the best sex they have had in fifty-four years. After a moment of thought she decided to give it a little bit of time so that she could find a way to tell him without scaring him or sending him into a panic, but she did want to talk to somebody, she needed help.

Ruby picked up the candle and went to see if the phones were still working. As she went she said a little prayer, and then prayed again that her prayer would be answered. She peeked into the bedroom, and was pleased to see that Cliff was just now getting out of bed and would still need a few minutes to get dressed. She went into the kitchen and picked up the phone, there was a dial tone.

"Thank you lord!" she said as she dialed 911.

2

The call came in at 4:10 as Erin and Todd waited out the storm inside of the ambulance. The rain continued to fall steadily, and came down so hard at times that it made it hard to see past the windshield, though right now there was but a drizzle spotting across the glass. The wind was blowing wildly and she could feel it gently rocking the ambulance from side to side. The murky color outside gave Erin an unsettling feeling in the pit of her stomach, but she supposed that it was probably the waiting that was getting to her. She hated working through storms like these. They always promised to be busy, trying, and exhausting. She tried to remember what it had been like working as a paramedic in Phoenix, and decided that she did not know how she had handled it. Things had been so much simpler for her since moving to the small town of Harvard, in Northern Illinois. There were no crack wars here, no murders, and no drive by shootings. Overall the people seemed to be much more relaxed, and except for the occasional bar fight, which was usually a welcome break from the routine spills and drills of ever day work, her job was rewarding and gratifying in a way that it had not been in Phoenix. Though right now they played a waiting game, and with storms like these things usually got weird no matter where you worked.

The call broke the silence like a scream. It made Erin jump, and awoke Todd from his nap as he sat behind the wheel.

"Rescue 1, you have a code blue at 211 Burr Oak Road. Do you copy?"

Todd's eyes snapped open and he reached for the transmitter, but as he brought his hand up to the console Erin began speaking.

"This is rescue 1 responding," Erin said casually.

Todd yawned as he rubbed the sleep from his eyes and then placed the ambulance in gear. He pulled out of the deserted Super Wash car wash parking lot and onto rural route 14, towards the address given over the radio. Sleepily he listened to the dispatcher as she relayed to them the pertinent details of the call.

"Go ahead Donna! We read you," Erin said with enthusiasm.

"Be advised," Donna began. "You have a seventy-nine year old female who is having acute chest pain with mild palpitations and extensive discomfort. She is conscious, alert and oriented at the moment, and states that she has taken a number of asprin. She has also taken several of her husband's nitroglycerine pills, and has been drinking wine. Know that she is a breast cancer survivor, and is currently on the usual meds. Last said to be stable, this could turn out to be nothing, but I don't think so, you guys better hurry."

"Ten-four," Erin said as she looked to Todd. "Let's hurry then."

Todd smiled to her as he turned on the ambulance lights and pulsed the siren to clear what little traffic there was on the flooded street. The rain began to fall harder as they passed over the viaduct and off of the main strip. They were only seven or so miles away from their patient, but the dense rain and wet streets were going to make it difficult to get there as fast as he would like. He was tired from a late night of band rehearsal, and although the rain made for tricky driving, he was just pleased that the call had not been a car accident or something worse. Of course, as emergencies went there weren't many calls as dire as a code blue, but it was still a routine call, and he knew what to expect.

Todd was a good emergency medical technician, but aside from whatever patient he might be treating, everything came second to his music. He played bass for his latest in a string of bands that did not challenge him. The one he was in now was no different, and reminded him that he needed to get out of this shitty little town that he had grown up in. He felt the need to be challenged, and he supposed that was why he loved emergency medicine, the unknown was always looming ahead waiting there ready to teach him something. Though as far as his music went he was left unfulfilled. He found it harder and harder to find a challenge in the young bands in which he found himself playing. He was too experienced to learn anything else in this isolated small farming community. Often he was expected to instruct and direct the young talent that he played with, though Todd was still eager to learn, and would not yet be satisfied by teaching others. Right now though, his mind was on other things, there was a woman out there that needed his help, and he was not the type of person who let people down.

"I know a shortcut," Todd said with a smile as he turned down a side street and headed away from town into the vast miles of corn-bordered roads beyond.

"Oh no," Erin said with a smile. "Not another one of your shortcuts."

"Come on," Todd chided. "Have I ever steered us wrong before? Besides, I live just a couple of miles from there. I could cut five minutes from our trip." He looked over at her as he awaited her response and noticed how her dark auburn hair shined in the strange light of the storm. Her soft pale skin reflected the ominous hues of the sky making her appear as if she was glowing. She was beautiful, intelligent, and sensual, and Todd could not help his

18

feelings for her. He had never shared his feelings with her, though he suspected that she knew. Erin was insightful and he believed that she was probably saving him from the embarrassment and the awkward situations that would undoubtedly arise if she were to know his true feelings and turn him down while they continued working together. He was okay with that and was happy enough just to work by her side. She was four years younger than he, though he found that he had much to learn, and she was a well of experience and knowledge. Besides, he had a rule about dating co-workers, though that did not keep his eyes from wandering occasionally.

"All right," Erin said apologetically. "We can go your way." She was being sarcastic and had every confidence that Todd could get them there faster by way of the back roads. They had been working together for just over a year and she trusted him beyond a shadow of a doubt. He was honest to a fault, a quality characteristic that she both abhorred as well as admired. He was also funny, and though a little bit strange she had developed a bond with him that she supposed most paramedics acquired with their partners. There was a part of her that believed that the bond went past the boundaries of a co-worker relationship, but she assumed that those feelings were but a product of her fanciful imagination and resided herself to merely enjoying his company on the job. Todd had waist long black hair in which he kept hidden beneath a ball cap while working; though in his off hours he was a talented musician with what could be a bright and promising future. What she knew most of all was that he was a good and caring person as well as a dedicated and knowledgeable emergency medical technician.

"You'll see," Todd proclaimed. "Seven miles in under ten minutes."

"Let's see it then!" she said encouraging him to prove himself.

"Okay," Todd said with a nod. He then turned on the sirens and pressed the accelerator to the floor. He then had to slow the ambulance to a crawl as the rain came down heavier than ever and he struggled to see past the windshield.

"You know, I have never seen weather like this. Have you?" Erin asked.

Todd shook his head. "No, actually I haven't, and I grew up here."

They traveled on like this for a few moments, and then the rain ceased. It stopped suddenly, almost as if god had turned off a faucet that he had forgotten was running.

Todd smiled. "The race is on!" he said enthusiastically and once again pressed the accelerator to the floor.

With the lights flashing and the sirens blaring they cruised down the country roads. There were six miles of farmland in between them and the woman in distress. They always took the straightest and shortest route, but Todd's daredevil driving in this stormy weather made her nerves tingle and she began to grow apprehensive. She knew that he drove these back roads daily, and that he was well experienced on driving the ambulance and she bit her tongue as they continued on. Though when the first of a series of sharp turns appeared ahead and he neglected to slow down, she decided to speak up.

"Slow down hero!" she said sharply. "We aren't going to be able to help anyone if you get us into an accident. Okay?"

Todd appeared to have not heard her and did not slow as they approached the first turn, but instead pushed down a little harder on the accelerator.

"Slow down!" she said again more urgently. "Todd!" she cursed.

Todd smiled as he tried to ignore her, and steered the ambulance into the turn. He had been driving down this street and around these turns for as long as he had been driving, and he knew what he was doing. He stopped smiling long enough to whistle a short melody as the ambulance glided smoothly and safely around the turn. When he looked back to her he found that she had an angry look in her eyes, though he could not help himself from laughing.

"I am sorry," he tried to say through his laughter. "I have never seen you so squeamish."

Erin tried to stay calm as she found herself nearing some kind of panic attack. Her heart was pounding vigorously and she could feel her asthma beginning to shorten her breaths. Forgetting about Todd's foolish driving and the treacherous rural road, she opened the fanny pack that she wore around her waist and retrieved her inhaler. All that she wanted and needed right then was to breath freely again, and she closed her eyes as she took three slow and deep breaths of the asthma medication.

Todd slowed the ambulance and his grin was replaced with a look of concern as he reached over and touched her on her shoulder. "Erin? Are you all right? You look kind of pale."

Erin's breath quickly began to return and she shook her head. "Yes, I am fine. I don't know what's wrong. I just have a bad feeling about this one, and you are driving like a fucking maniac!" she exclaimed.

Todd blushed. "Sorry, I didn't mean to scare you."

"Yes you did!" she snapped back at him.

Todd couldn't help but start laughing again, and this time Erin cracked a smile also. "Well maybe I tried to scare you a little, but I didn't mean to send you into an asthma attack."

"I know," she said softly. "I think that this storm has just got me spooked a little."

"A little?" Todd asked as his laughter dwindled to a smile.

"Okay, maybe a bit more than a little," she acknowledged. "I just want to get this call over with as quickly as possible."

Todd was about to say that if she would let him drive a little faster they would get there sooner, but he decided to keep his thoughts to himself. She seemed different today. She was as focused as always, though more distant than usual. He chose not to press her about it, but they did have a job to do. He slowed the ambulance, but not much.

Erin wasn't quite sure of why she was so jumpy today, and was surprised to find her right hand clutching the door handle so tightly that her knuckles had turned white. In her other hand she clenched onto her inhaler as if for her life. Her heart was racing, and as she looked to the speed gage she decided that it had nothing to do with Todd's driving as they were only going forty-five miles an hour. Doing her best to try to calm herself she closed her eyes for a moment. She began to take another breath of her inhaler, but when she opened her eyes she saw that the road beyond the second turn disappeared underneath a river of water.

"Look out!" she screamed as she noticed that Todd was watching her rather than the road ahead.

"What?" he started to ask as he looked back to the road in front of him and then cursed when he saw the watery obstacle in their path.

"Oh shit!" he yelled as he hit the breaks and the tires hydroplaned over the roads wet surface. Instinctively he tried to pump the breaks but it was useless and the ambulance began to spin. In an attempt to control the spin he wrenched the steering wheel in one direction and then the other, but that did little if anything. Without any control they spun into the floods swift current so hard and fast that Todd was sure that the ambulance was going to tip over, but as they entered into the flooded section of roadway the rushing water brought them to a stuttered halt and the engine died.

Shaken and stirred, Todd looked over to Erin and saw that she was so pale that she appeared ghostly. "Are you all right?" he asked numbly.

Erin shook her head yes, but she wasn't quite sure. She had a scream caught in her throat and she was afraid that if she spoke it might break free. Her hands were still clutching the door handle and inhaler, though so tightly now that her fingers hurt. Within her head she could feel the accelerated pounding of her heart as waves of adrenalin passed through her blood stream causing her to feel dizzy and a little bit nauseous.

All was quiet now. With the engine dead the only sounds were that of the light rain falling on the ambulance roof, a low thunder rumbling from the distance, and the reverberation of Todd's rapid breathing. They had spun a complete 180 degrees, and were now facing the direction in which they had come.

Erin thought that perhaps she had been more traumatized than she had thought as she sensed the whole world rocking back and forth, but then realized that it was merely the waters strong current that was rocking the ambulance from side to side. She looked to Todd as she took another breath from her inhaler and found that he was shaking.

"Jesus Todd, this is some shortcut," she said quietly.

Todd shook his head as he fought to calm his nerves. "I have never seen this road flood like this. Ever! Really!"

"Okay," Erin said slowly. "So what now? Are we stuck?"

Todd shrugged his shoulders as he tried to steady his shaky hand and reached for the ignition. "I hope not," he said as he turned the key to the off position and then tried to restart the ambulance. The engine started immediately, springing to life along with the siren, which made both of them jump nearly out of their skins. Todd quickly shut off the siren and then smiled at Erin.

"Thank god," Erin said with a sigh of relief.

"No, you can thank the lord in a minute. We are not out of this yet," Todd said as he placed the ambulance in gear and slowly depressed the accelerator. Nothing happened.

"Dam it!" he shouted as he changed gears struggling to find enough traction on the flooded road. He put the transmission in first gear and the vehicle lurched and slowly began to move forwards, though the current was strong and began pulling ambulance sideways.

Erin let go of the door handle and crossed her fingers, though it didn't do any good and the tires began spinning once again. "So what are we supposed to do now? Radio for help?"

"Not yet," Todd said as he placed the transmission in park. "I am going to step out and see what we are looking at."

Erin shook her head. "What? Are you crazy?" she asked. Having grown up in Arizona she knew that flash floods were extremely dangerous, and often deadly. In the desert they were a common and respected menace of nature, and she knew well enough to steer clear of them when and if you had a choice, and they had a choice.

"Todd, you can't go out there!" she sternly advised. "You are going to get yourself killed."

Todd smiled at her as he opened the door. "I will be back in a minute," he said.

Erin smiled back at him disapprovingly. "Oh yeah, weren't those Custards famous last words?"

Todd shook his head and grinned at her as he slid out of the door and into the rain. The water was running past his ankles as he stood on the running boards, and he found that he wasn't quite sure how he should proceed. Slowly he stepped down into the icy cold water, first with his left leg, and then his right. The water came to just past his knees; though the current was so strong that it rose to his waist as it pushed against him. He closed the driver side door behind him and looked towards the back of the ambulance. He was hoping to find something in which he could use to help the ambulance regain some of the lost traction on the flooded roadway, but all he saw was the rushing water. He briefly wondered what he had been thinking to come out there, but decided that he would just take a quick look to make sure that there was nothing that could be done. Carefully he began to make his way to the rear of the vehicle, though after only a few steps the water's swift current carried his feet out from underneath of him.

The strength of the current was unbelievably immense as it took control of him and pulled him down. He let out a startled yell as he tried uselessly to regain his footing and was sucked underneath its shallow surface. His body spun in one direction and then another, twisting and spinning like a rag doll in a washing machine. He bleakly wondered if he was going to die here, like this, in three feet of water. He struggled to find the surface as the overwhelming current carried him down stream. It was all that he could do not to take a breath of the frigid water as his lungs ached for air. His mind was swimming inside of a cloud of confusion as he could no longer distinguish which way was up nor down. He felt strangely exhilarated, as his bloodstream was flooded with adrenalin and endorphins. This sensation was accompanied by an unimaginable terror in which he had only known in his dreams, and he hoped that this was one of them.

Just when Todd decided that he could hold his breath no longer, his body became ensnared in a tangle of fallen branches and debris that had gathered several yards past the shoulder of the road. His head popped up out of the water and he gasped for breath as he grasped onto the branches for dear life.

His ball cap had come off allowing his long black hair to streak across his face as it stirred in the water around him. He was shivering both from the cold as well as from the paralyzing fear of death that lingered inside of him as he stayed there clutching the branches and debris. There were a million things racing through his mind, though first and foremost he thought about the old lady that was having a heart attack not too far from here, and at this moment he coldly empathized with her, as he had just had a taste of what she must be feeling. After taking a moment to catch his breath he began moving towards the bank of the water using the tangle of branches for support as he went.

Erin unbuckled her safety belt and climbed into the drivers seat. She looked out of the windows and into the mirrors, but could not see any sign of Todd. She was worried for him, but supposed that the water was not yet high enough to be deadly, then again she knew that one really couldn't tell just by looking. Through her training as a paramedic she knew that a strong undertow could drag a person away in mere seconds, and she once again looked for him but could not see anything but the swiftly flowing water.

Alone she sat there listening to the gentle rain and rhythmic squeaking of the windshield wipers. It only took a moment for her grow impatient, and she decided to try her hand at driving the ambulance out of the water. She placed her foot on the break and put the ambulance in gear. Ever so slowly she released the break and lightly tapped on the accelerator. Nothing happened, as she had expected, though she had to try. She then decided to try moving in reverse and again placed her foot upon the break and placed the transmission in reverse. She had no intention of driving any farther into to water, as it appeared to get deeper further on, she just wanted to see if it would work. Slowly she released the break and this time something happened. The tires began spinning as she thought they would, but then they caught something and the ambulance lurched backwards.

"Oops," Erin said with a smile, surprised that she had gotten the ambulance to move at all. She quickly hit the break, and then placed the gearshift in drive once again. Her palms were growing sweaty with nervous tension, and she wiped them on her legs of her light blue jumpsuit. She didn't feel comfortable out here near the middle of the water, which looked to her as if it was getting deeper by the minute. There wasn't anything that Todd was

29

going to be able to do for them outside, that she was sure of, so she supposed that if there was a chance that she could drive the ambulance out of this mess, she should take it. There were risks involved, she knew that if the current caught the ambulance and pushed sideways past the shoulder of the road the ambulance was likely to tip over, as there were large drainage ditches on either side of the street. Left with no other choice she quickly let off of the break and slowly depressed the accelerator. This time the ambulance moved, more than that, it bounced as if it had just run over something large. Erin immediately thought of Todd as she continued to make her way forwards towards the edge of the water. Once again she searched for him. She frantically peered through the windows and mirrors hoping to see him waiting for her safely out of the way, though once again he was nowhere to be seen. Swarm upon swarm, butterflies began to flutter into her bowels, and she felt a swelling sense of impending doom that assured her that she had just killed Todd. She had run him over; pulling him down into the water while the immense weight of the ambulance purged the oxygen from his lungs. His spine rendered twisted and torn as she pulled the flesh away from his bones with spinning tires. Erin shook her head as she tried to repel the vivid unwanted images of Todd's stricken corps from her imagination. Though not until he was found could she vanquish them, and they seemed more realistic than ever as the minutes ticked by.

Slowly the ambulance continued to creep forward until Erin had driven out of the water, and out of danger. Still, she felt no relief, as she feared for Todd's life, afraid that she had killed him. She quickly parked the ambulance and got out to search for him. The rain was cold and getting heavier by the second, though she felt little of it as she was consumed with worry. Tears made their way down her face as she walked up to the water and he was nowhere to be found. There was literally no sign of him, and she began to panic. The rain continued to fall harder and harder still, until Erin could see little of anything in the channel of water.

Todd walked out of the icy water more than fifty yards down stream and was shocked to see that Erin was driving the ambulance out of the flooded roadway.

"Oh dam!" he said as he tried to imagine what he must look like right now, and felt foolish. He could picture Erin in his mind, laughing at him as he emerged from the water like a scrawny creature of the black lagoon or something, and he shook his head and smiled in spite of himself. Shivering and shaken he walked back through the rain as it poured down, though he hardly noticed it, as he was already soaked. A grin creased his lips as he watched Erin as she got out of the ambulance and walked up to the water. It was then that he realized that she had not yet seen him, and he could only imagine of what she must be thinking.

"Todd!" Erin screamed as she walked up and down the waters edge calling out his name. There was a growing sense of panic gnawing at her, and though she chocked them back with all of her might, she knew that she was close to tears.

"Dam it Todd! Answer me!" she screamed to no avail as she made one last attempt to locate him. When she could still not find him the tears began, and she turned to go back to the ambulance to radio for help. As she turned she kept her eyes on the water and did not see Todd as she walked right into him, and he scared the living hell out of her.

She gasped in shock as she gazed into his eyes, and several different emotions passed through her as she tried to recognize just how she felt.

"Dam you Todd!" she cursed and slapped him twice across the chest, and the tears ran freely. "Dam you!" she said again as she then hugged him tightly and let him comfort her fears.

Todd hugged her back, and as he did all of his discomfort vanished. Here in his arms was this warm and beautiful woman in which he had dreamed of holding for so long, though now as his dream came true he found the circumstances around them not at all like he had fantasized, but the feeling was the same. He longed for her more than anything. More than the music that he played, more than their partnership that his feelings betrayed, and at that moment he forgot about the elderly woman who waited in peril for their arrival. As they slowly separated at met each other's eyes he could not tell if she was crying, or it was merely the rain, but wiped the water away never the less. Her gaze was warm and entrancing, and he found that he could not turn away. Feeling that he had lost all control over himself he leaned in gently, and kissed her softly upon the lips. As he did this he felt a stirring in his groin that he knew was even more inappropriate than the kiss, though he had even less control over that. Pulling away slowly he saw an expression on her face like he had never seen before. She had a most intense look that made him half expect her to slap him across the face, although he could not tell what she was thinking.

Erin felt overwhelmed, first by Todd's abrupt disappearance in the water, and then again by his fragile kiss. She found her mind spinning, though she welcomed his touch, and when he pulled away and she looked into his eyes she found herself hungry for more, and returned his kiss deeply. He did not fight it, as she knew he would not. She had sensed the attraction that they had shared for some time now, though neither of them had dared express their feelings, that is until now. This expression of love that they shared was long over due, and had been longed for by both. And now that it was no longer hidden they gave into their feelings and held each other closely. When the kiss was over they reluctantly released each other, and though neither of them regretted what had happened they both felt a little bit uncomfortable of their spontaneous behavior.

"I thought that you were dead," Erin said quietly as a crash of thunder echoed over the landscape.

"Dam near," Todd replied. "For a moment there I thought I was going to…." He decided not to finish the sentence and shook his head. "It doesn't matter. I am fine now. Better than ever in fact," he said with a smile.

Erin shook her head with a smile. "Me too, but we still have a job to do."

"Right!" Todd acknowledged as he remembered that the passing of time could be fatal, and they quickly returned to the ambulance.

Erin climbed into the drivers seat as Todd walked to the passenger door and slid in. They both had a feeling of relief as they had made it through this ordeal unscathed, and were anxious to get moving as much for the fact that they were on the job, and someone's life was at stake, as for the reason that they wanted to get this call over with so they could express their feelings for each other that had long been neglected.

"Which way now?" Erin asked as she backtracked away from the flooded roadway and towards town.

Todd tried to look thoughtful as he tied his wet hair back into a ponytail. "Let's try state line road," he said as he finished his hair and began to dry off with one of the blankets that the ambulance carried. "I have never seen state line flood before."

Erin nodded. "State line it is then." She turned on the lights and sirens once again, and sped up until she feared that she might lose control. Though she felt much more comfortable at this speed with her behind the wheel. Still, she had a premonition that somewhere, somehow, something disastrous lay ahead, and putting her own fears aside she thought of the patient, anxiously waiting, desperately praying, and went ahead regardless of her own intuitions.

They retraced their path along the back roads, and turned onto route 14. They were now three miles away from State Line road, which was the street that separated Southern Wisconsin from Northern Illinois. It had now been more than fifteen minutes since the call had come in, and they feared that they would not be able to get to their patient in time, as they were still more than ten minutes away.

Erin did not blame Todd for their slow pace, for if the circumstances had been different and the weather less inclement she knew that they would probably have been there by now. There were some things that no one could control, the passing of time, and the patterns of weather being two of them.

"Donna?" Todd said as he picked up the transmitter from the console radio and called for the dispatcher. "Donna, this is rescue

1, do you copy?" There was no reply, and the only sound they heard were the constant bursts of static that was caused by the lightning that was occurring from all around them. He shrugged his shoulders as she gave Erin an uneasy glance and tried again.

"Donna! This is rescue 1 do you read me? We had some trouble do you copy?"

"Rescue 1 please hold," Donna answered, and the radio again sounded of static.

"This is weird," Erin stated as she passed an old pick up truck that had pulled over to let them by. "She has never put us on hold before."

Todd shrugged his shoulders and was about to say something when Donna called back over the radio.

"Rescue one, are you guys all right?" Donna asked fearfully.

"Yeah, we are okay," Todd answered. "We almost got stuck in the river on Ramer road is all."

There was a moment of silence before Donna replied. "There isn't a river on Ramer road," Donna said skeptically.

Todd almost laughed. "Well there is now. Is there any word on the code blue? We had to re-route and are a couple of minutes behind schedule."

"Afraid not," Donna acknowledged. "She was still stable a few minutes ago, but the phone lines have since gone out, but that isn't the half of it. There have been tornados spotted in that area, so you be careful! There had been several calls regarding them, though there is, as of yet no information about damage or injuries. Just the same this looks like it might turn out to be one hell of a night. Do you guys see anything where you are now?"

Erin and Todd both looked outside at the storm around them. The color of the sky had turned into a greenish orange canopy that looked more like a strange painting rather than real life. It had stopped raining where they were, though they could see that the rain was falling heavily in the west. They searched all around them but could see no signs of a tornado. Erin's stomach tightened as she half expected to see a twister blossom from the sky above and consume them hungrily. She told herself that she was being silly, and tried not to let her imagination get the better of her. She shrugged her shoulders to say that she saw nothing, and concentrated on the road ahead.

"No, we don't see anything over here," Todd answered. "We are almost to State Line road."

"State Line road had been detoured to route 67 due to flooding," Donna warned.

"Dam!" Todd said to himself. "Thanks Donna," he said as they passed their intended turn and continued on to route 67. "We will keep you informed."

"Okay," Donna replied. "And you guys be careful!"

"Tornado's," Erin said with an ominous tone. "Have you ever seen one?"

Todd shook his head. "Yes and no. I have seen a funnel cloud, quite a few of them in fact, but they aren't considered tornados until they touch the ground. We don't get too many of them up here. Usually they stay further to the south. Have you?" He asked.

"Me? No," she said. I don't think that I have even ever heard of one in Arizona. Dust storms yes, but not tornados. We do get these things called dust devils that look kind of like tornados, but on a much smaller scale, and they lack any kind of damaging strength."

"Dust devils huh, that might be a good name for a band," said Todd with a smile.

Their turn came into view just as the rain began to fall heavily once again, and regrettably they had to slow down once more. The detour to 67 meant that they would have to pass through the tiny town of Sharon Wisconsin, and then back into Illinois to reach the callers location. This would add a few more precious minutes to their time, and time was often the essence of life that passed on calls such as these.

Erin went as fast as she could safely go as gusts of wind threatened to blow her off course and from the road. She held the wheel steadily and was nearing the Sharon city limits when the first twister came into view less than a mile away.

3

Ruby meadows place the phone back onto the hook just as Cliff walked out of the bedroom and into the kitchen. She tried to act casual as if there was nothing out of the ordinary happening even though it was difficult. She didn't know how long it would take for the paramedics to arrive, and wasn't at all sure about how she should tell Cliff that they were coming. He would be terribly worried, and she did not want to scare him. Deep inside she prayed that it was merely a case of indigestion, gas, or something else just as innocent. She tried to tell herself that there was nothing to be scared of, even if it is a heart attack, people had heart attacks all the time and most of them live, a few extra medicines, a change of diet, that's what would happen in the end, that is what she hoped. Still, the ambulance had been dispatched, and would be here shortly. Her discomfort continued, though it did not seem as severe as it had before, and she hoped that the nitro, and asprin would see her through. Right now there was only a mild ache in her chest, and she tried not to be too concerned for Cliff's sake.

"Who was that on the phone?" Cliff asked as he served himself up a plate full of meat and potatoes.

"It was a wrong number," Ruby hesitantly lied.

"I didn't even hear the phone ring," he commented before taking a bite of his roast.

"That is because it didn't," she confessed, and then took a long drink of her wine. Cliff was looking at her questioningly while he chewed his food, and she decided not to tiptoe around the truth any further. "Okay," she said. "Now please don't get upset or anything, but I think that I might be having a heart attack, and that was 911 on the phone. There is an ambulance on the way." A tear leaked out of the corner of her eye as she finished, and she fought to hold back the emotion that was swelling within her, threatening to overcome the stern composure in which she had steadied herself. She felt that by telling Cliff, she had accepted the horror of the truth herself, and with acceptance came fear as she realized the magnitude of what was happening to her.

"Oh my god!" Cliff said as he got up from the table and went to her side and held her. "What can I do? Is there anything that I can do?"

Ruby could see the concern take shape in her husbands face, and that only made the tears fall faster as she tried to say that everything would be all right.

"No, you are fine, and I will be okay too," she said before she bit her tongue and tried to control her emotions. "The paramedics will be here any minute. They will know what to do."

"Are you sure?" he asked. "Can I get you something? Do you want to lie down?"

"No thank you," she said with a smile that was true and warm. "And I think that I feel better sitting up. Besides, I took some asprin and a few of your nitro pills, and I think that I feel better. I think that they helped. Hell, this could all turn out to be nothing. Right?"

Cliff took her hands into his and pulled them softly around him. She leaned in closely and rested her head upon his chest. He said nothing now as he fought to conceal his own tears in an attempt to be strong for her. Together they stood in the dim candlelight waiting for the rescue squad that was surely on its way.

4

"Look!" Erin shouted as the thin whispery funnel cloud spun into sight. "There! I see one! There!" She shrieked as she pointed out of the window past Todd into the distance beyond.

Todd thought that Erin's eyeballs were going to pop out of their sockets, though as he followed her finger to the right side of the ambulance he spotted the terrifying vortex that was ripping apart everything that was in it's path. His pulse began to quicken, and his mouth went dry as his mind went blank, and he tried to think of what they should do.

"What should we do Todd?" Erin asked franticly.

"Stay away from it!" Todd answered excitedly.

She shook her head. "No shit! I can't tell which way it's going! Can you?"

He shrugged his shoulders. "Just a second," he said as he peered through the window trying to distinguish in which direction it was heading in. "I think that it's moving away from us."

"You think? Are you sure?"

"Yeah, I think so. I am almost positive." It suddenly stopped raining, and he rolled down the window to get a better look. "No! It is moving in the same direction that we are. I am sure of it, but it isn't heading towards us!" He called out with his head half way out the window.

Erin tried to keep her eyes focused on the road, but could not help herself from staring at the tornado as it made its way through the tall cornfield next to them. She hoped that Todd was right, and that the twister wasn't coming at them, for she still could not tell exactly which way it was moving. Her palms had grown sweaty and her nerves were on fire, as she grew dizzy with fear. Brilliant streaks of lightning pierced the sky with beautiful shards of color, and amidst all of the terror she found a fascinating beauty in the storm that she had not noticed before.

"Oh no!" Todd shrieked disturbingly with his head and shoulders still hanging out of the window. "Go! Go! Hurry up Erin!"

"What is it?" She called back to him afraid to find out what it was.

"It's coming! I was wrong! It's coming!" He shouted. "It is right behind us! GO! Go! Go!"

Erin almost squealed in terror as she hit the gas and looked into the side mirror to see how close it was. What she saw made her jaw drop, and her body tremble with fear. A wall of debris a half of a mile wide was less than a mile behind them, and gaining quickly. They were traveling close to sixty miles an hour as they entered the town of Sharon. There was no other traffic on the road, and she looked back once again and saw that the tornado was closer that it had been just moments ago. She feared that they would not be able to outrun the monstrous twister, and looked back to the road intent on finding someplace in which they could safely hide until it passed. But as she looked back to the road she saw a little boy running into the street in front of them. She had but only a fraction of a second to respond, and in that short segment of time she realized that there was almost no way to avoid hitting the child, though she would do what she could.

"Oh shit!" Erin screamed as she cut the wheel and hit the breaks to avoid hitting the child. She cut the wheel sharply, which sent the ambulance into a spin that caused the vehicle to roll over, very nearly crushing the boy.

Halfway through the spin Todd was thrown from the vehicle window and disappeared from Erin's sight. It was than that the ambulance crashed onto its side, brutally throwing her against the windshield and steering wheel. Dazed and disoriented she tried to shield herself from the shattering glass as the ambulance slid along the pavement, and then stopped abruptly after colliding with a light pole outside of the town elementary school.

She wasn't sure of what had happened after trying to miss the child in the street. She didn't know if the tornado had caught up to them, or they had simply crashed. Right now all that she knew was that she could no longer feel or move her legs. She lay in a crumpled heap on the shattered passenger side widow writhing in agony. There was blood splatter over everything, though she could not tell where it had come from, so much blood. The pain in her back was excruciating, and she fought against the dizziness that was swimming over her threatening to steal her consciousness away. Tears began to leak out of her eyes as she struggled against the pain trying to make her broken body obey her commands, but the pain was too much, and her bones were in no position to listen. It was then that she heard the unmistakable whirling thunder of the twister that was quickly approaching.

"Oh Christ!" she thought out loud. As if the crash wasn't enough, the tornado was sure to finish her off. She began to say a silent prayer, and as if sent from heaven the boy she had nearly run over appeared. He stared at her through the shattered windshield with a look of innocence that made him appear younger than his age. He was wet and dirty, though his eyes shown of a sense of peace, and lacked any fear of the approaching tornado as he knelt down to look at her through the jagged remains of the windshield.

"Can you help me find my mommy?" The young child asked.

In spite of her pain Erin smiled through her tears. The boy looked about six years old, and had short hair. His fair skin seemed to glow in the unusual light of the storm, and his voice was soothing and soft. He wore an old looking baseball jersey, and slacks that had been cut off to make shorts, and didn't seem to notice the weather, chill, or danger that he was in.

She shook her head. "No boy. I am kind of a mess here. "You go and find someplace safe. Quickly now! There is a tornado coming. Your mom would want you to be safe."

The boy looked over his shoulder to the tornado, though appeared unconcerned by it. He then looked back to Erin. "My name is Bobby. Can you help me find my mommy? She needs me. My daddy too."

Erin shook her head and winced as a fresh jolt of pain rocked through her. She could feel her lungs beginning to close up as her asthma resurfaced and threatened to choke off her oxygen. "No!" she cried with fresh tears. "Listen, I would if I could, but I can't! So get the fuck out of here! Run Boy! Run as fast as you can! Go get help!"

Instead of leaving the child reached through the hole where the windshield had been and firmly grasped her hand.

Erin knew the position she was in, she knew what was coming, and she wanted nothing more than to get this child out of danger. She was done for, but this boy had a chance if he would only go away, find a place to escape the tornado's wrath. He had a chance, she did not.

When bobby reached for her hand she tried to pull away, but she did not have the strength. And when he touched her, something happened. He gripped her hand, and right away she noticed that he was surprisingly strong for his age. His grip was like iron, and somehow seemed to be vibrating. The vibrations ran into and through her and she grew numb as they shook her soul. She closed her eyes. Things seemed to change in that moment, as she became disoriented and her perceptions distorted. The pain that she felt disappeared along with the fear and uncertainty of what was happening around her. When she opened her eyes once again she felt both energized and whole, though the sound was both deafening as well as enlightening. It sounded as if she were inside of a vacuum, and she quickly recovered her senses. Bobby was still there holding onto her hand. She could see him mouthing the words "Can you help me find my mommy?" Though she could not hear him over the tornado that was almost on top of them.

Right away she sensed feeling in her legs, and with slow uncertainty she began to move them, and found that she could. In fact she didn't feel any injuries at all. With a quick look at herself she surmised that somehow she was all right, that she wasn't as bad off as she had thought. She didn't know how that could be possible with so much blood everywhere. It was then that she thought of Todd and feared the worst. Her concern was quickly averted as debris from the tornado began swirling around them venomously.

She took hold of Bobby's arm and pulled him through the shattered windshield and into the ambulance. Pulling the child along she scrambled into the back of the ambulance where she would have normally treated her patients, and braced for the twisters impact.

It started with what Erin could only describe as a vicious earthquake. The ambulance shook and trembled, and then quickly began to spin savagely as Erin and Bobby held each other as well as anything stable that they could hold on to, but mostly they held onto each other, and did so as if their lives depended on it. It sounded to her as if a train was being driven straight through the ambulance. The wind was ravenous as it tore at the ambulance with incredible force. All of the blankets, gauze, and other medical essentials were spinning and whipping through the air, some with dangerous ferocity. Erin did her best to shield both herself and

Bobby from the flying projectiles inside, while objects that had been caught up into the tornados fury slammed into the outside of the ambulance with the sound of thunder as they too were tossed asunder. At one point a pitchfork pierced through the shell of the ambulance nearly skewering them both, while leaving a gash in the vehicle wall allowing even more of the fierce winds into the back. It was then that the ambulance began to spin.

Erin screamed as the vehicle was spun and began rolling over. She tried to cushion the boy with the softness of her body, though as the ambulance began to tumble and spin it was impossible for her to hold onto him without crushing him under her own weight as they tumbled inside like two shoes inside of a clothes dryer. They were separated as they crashed against the roof, walls and floor of the vehicle. She thought that she wasn't doing enough to protect him, that there should be some kind of protocol for instances such as these, but she could not think of one. Only the thought of self preservation came to mind, that if she were not left alive to help those in need, than all could be lost. It wasn't any kind of consolation to her at the moment, but it was all that she could think of as the ambulance continued to roll and spin. She did not know how many times the ambulance had flipped and rolled but the shock of what was happening outweighed any sense of pain that she felt, and with a prayer that lasted but a split second she prayed for it to end.

Finally the ambulance lurched, spun, and crashed into something solid, and then came to rest. The wind and noise slowly began to diminish as everything inside of the back fell down onto the side of the wall where she and the ambulance had landed.

"Bobby!" Erin called out as she went to him. "Bobby! Are you all right? Can you hear me?" She called out finding him only a few feet from where she lay. She went to the child, brushing away the debris that was scattered on top of him. Bobby was lying motionless on the ambulance side, and with tears of fear she gently turned him over. He laid motionless in her arms as she cried, not caring so much that she was alive, she felt for a pulse and found none. It was then that her determination pushed her, her guilt arose and she buried it deep inside of her. This was not her fault! She told herself.

"NO!" she screamed. "It's not going to end this way!" She cleared a place on the floor (Which was the wall of the ambulance) and laid his body there. Ever so gently she placed her hand behind the child's neck and breathed a lungful of air into his body. His chest rose and fell, as she knew it must, though that was all and she laid him flat preparing to initiate CPR. She then placed her hands in the necessary point along his sternum and prepared herself to push when he opened his eyes.

Bobby began to pull himself up into a sitting position even before she realized what was happening. When she did realize that he was alive she looked him over carefully and was surprised to find that he didn't have a scratch on him. It was then that she remembered that she (by all rites) should be dead now herself, yet she was without injury also. She then pulled Bobby into her arms and held him tightly as fresh tears of joy streamed down her face.

"Please don't cry," said Bobby as he wiped some of her tears away with the palm of his hand. "We have to find my mommy and daddy. Fast."

"Okay sweetie," Erin said as she set the boy down and looked around the ambulance. "We will find them, I promise," she said as she reached over, and with some difficulty opened the lower door of the vehicle that was lying on its side.

As the door fell open she gasped as she found herself looking out at the remains of a destroyed classroom. "Oh my god!" she said stunned by the destruction she saw. The tornado had thrown the ambulance into and through one of the elementary school walls, and half way into a classroom. The rest of the school was all but demolished and looked as if it might be some ancient relic of an era long since past. It was in utter ruins, and left Erin in awe. She couldn't have imagined what would have happened had it not been summer time and these empty classrooms had been occupied, full of children. Erin realized that as bad as it was, this horrific tragedy could have been much worse and the loss that much more heart sickening.

Erin wondered how it was that they had survived the last ten minutes or so. She then looked to Bobby as he climbed out of the twisted ambulance and into the remains of the classroom. There was something special about him. He had performed a miracle, he had saved her life, and although she knew this to be true she began to question the validity of that explanation. Had she really been paralyzed? Was she really broken up so badly? She wondered if perhaps her recollection had been impaired by the traumatic events leading up to her miraculous recovery. The pain was not imagined, she knew that, but the pain was gone now and she was left mystified by the experience. She decided to worry about explanations later, right now there would be many who would need the kind of help she was trained to give, not to mention Bobby, the little miracle who had somehow saved her life.

Erin followed Bobby out of the ambulance and into the schoolroom. She grew a bit dizzy as she surveyed the damage that the tornado had done to the building, it was destruction, total and complete. There was no longer a roof covering the school, and most of the walls had been blown over or fallen down. There were books and papers strewn everywhere. Chairs and desks lay scattered in mangled, twisted heaps. She noticed a dead cow in one corner of the room, it's head cocked at an awful angle. Much of its hide had been stripped from its corpse leaving a grotesque carcass that made her turn away.

Erin carefully walked around the scattered debris towards the collapsed wall where the ambulance had come to rest. Bobby moved a bit faster and was already outside when he turned back to her.

"We must hurry! My mommy will be waiting," he said as he ran out of sight.

"Wait!" Erin hollered as she rushed to catch up with him. There was a light drizzle and a steady wind, but no sign of the tornado that had just passed. She spotted Bobby by the crossroads in front of the school waiting for her and she quickly jogged over to him. As she went she wondered why she was not hearing the towns tornado siren, and suspected that it was not in working order, or the twister had destroyed it. In either case, the town's people laid in the path of nature's wrath, unknowing of the horror that was about to change their lives forever.

The school was set upon a small rise, the top of which was the crossroads, and there, Bobby stood looking over the small town of Sharon.

"Hey!" Erin said as she reached him, but lost her voice when she saw what Bobby was looking at. There were five tornados that she could see from the hilltop. Only one of them was touching the ground, as the other four hung over the town like stalagmites in a cave. "Dear god!" She said as the reality of what was happening, and what she had lived through began to set in. Noticing that

Bobby was looking at her she returned the glance, and tried to smile. He smiled back as he reached up and took her hand.

Once again, Bobby's touch had a strange, almost mind altering effect on Erin. Her perceptions of reality became distorted in ways that she could not comprehend or explain, and she shook her head in an attempt to clear the cobwebs from her mind as she tried to figure out what it was that was happening. Things just seemed to appear different, more vivid; multidimensional was the word that came to her mind, though everything was still the same. Then as she followed Bobby's gaze back to the tornados she found what she was looking for. The sky seemed darker and more threatening, and the tornados no longer appeared to be what she knew they were. What she saw made her blood run cold, and sent shivers running along her spine. The clouds in which the tornados sprung had folded themselves into a shape of a withered hand, and the tornados had become long sinister fingers that ended with claws that reached down and scorched the earth.

Erin quickly pulled her hand away from Bobby's, and instantly everything returned to normal, or at least as normal as things were before he had touched her. The tornados were just tornados, and there was no hand hovering within the clouds. She looked down at Bobby and was about to ask who, or what he was, when he began running again, down the hill and towards the tornados.

"Come on Erin! They will be waiting," he called out to her as he went.

"Wait Bobby! It is too dangerous right now!" She yelled as she started after him, and then slowed as she cast a hopeful glance around the area looking for Todd who she feared could not have survived such a terrible accident, and even worse tornado. She then remembered all of the blood that had covered the passenger side of the ambulance and closed her eyes as new tears leaked from them. Fearing the worst for Todd, and knowing that there would probably be nothing that she could do for him now, she hurried after Bobby, all the while wondering how he had known her name.

Erin followed after Bobby as he ran down the street towards the twisters, and the wreckage that they had left in their wake. He seemed to be oblivious to the danger that he was in, and almost appeared to be chasing after the tornado that had nearly claimed their lives. He had said that he was looking for his mother. But who was she? Erin didn't know. She knew very few people who lived in the town of Sharon, and didn't have a clue as to where to start looking. Above all she wanted to keep Bobby out of danger, but to do that she had to catch him first.

As Erin ran to catch up with the boy the rain began falling heavily once again. She was wet and the rain was cold, though she felt none of it. Her mind was plagued by thoughts of what she should have or could have done, and though she knew that there was no help for what had happened thus far she could not escape the feeling that the loss of Todd had somehow been her fault. She wanted to stop and look for him, to see if there was anything that she could do, but she knew that it was more than likely that he had not survived and she was sure that he would have wanted her to help the child. So she tried to ignore the *(what if)* questions that were floating around in her head, and focused instead on what she could do now to help those she could.

She had Questions for Bobby that only he could answer. Where did he live? Where was he going? How had he healed her? She especially wanted to know the latter.

The wind gusts were so strong that Erin thought that she might actually be blown over more than once. Bobby seemed to have no trouble with the weather, and like everything else appeared not to notice, or not to care.

As Erin ran to him she saw that he was heading towards a house that was the first in a series of homes that had been nearly destroyed by the twister as it cut it's swath of destruction through the neighborhood. This particular house appeared to have sustained considerably more damage than the others, and looked as if the wind blew the wrong way it would topple to the ground. It was a large two-story home that had gray aluminum siding, though most of it had been stripped from the walls. There were numerous gaping holes where the tornado had ripped out chunks of wall and possibly a support beam or two as it was left leaning ominously to the left.

"No Bobby! Don't go in there!" She called to him, though he paid no attention to her and ran up the steps of the porch and disappeared into the house.

Erin caught up to him as he stood just inside of the entranceway to the home, and she snatched up his arm and turned him around. "No Bobby! This isn't safe," she said as she began to lead him away.

"No!" The boy protested as he pulled his arm free.

"Is this your house Bobby? Is this where you live?"

"No," Bobby said as he shook his head. "But she is calling me. Can't you hear her?"

"Who is calling you? Your mother?" Erin inquired skeptically. Bobby shook his head no, though almost as if in answer to her question she heard moaning and crying coming from someplace inside of the house.

The house was as dark as dusk and filled with shadows. Erin knew that the sun would not be setting for another three hours, but the thick clouds choked off the sunlight from above like her asthma did the air from her lungs. It was then that she realized that after all of the traumatic events brought about by the tornado she had run nearly a block as fast as she could, and although she was a little out of breath, she showed no signs of having any asthmatic symptoms. Normally she would have had to stop half way through a run like that to breathe from her inhaler, but had not needed to. She smiled at the thought of being free from such a problematic ailment. Had Bobby cured her, she wondered, she did not know. All that she knew was that something extraordinary had happened to her, and the mystery seemed to be growing more puzzling by the minute. She let the revelation slip to the back of her thoughts as she listened to the sounds of anguish emanating from somewhere inside of the house. Right now all that mattered was helping those who were sure to be in jeopardy due to the tornado, and for the first time since she could remember her life help purpose. She found a reason for where she was at in her life, and aside from the boy, everything made sense.

Together Erin and Bobby walked through the wreckage of the house searching for the source of the crying. Stepping around rain soaked furniture and destroyed belongings they walked through the rubble of the once beautiful home. Erin noticed several family pictures that lay scattered in the debris and smiled sadly for the people who had lost their home, and quite possibly their lives.

It wasn't long before they came across the tattered body of a young girl that looked to be only a few years older than bobby. She had long dark hair that was saturated with blood, and a head wound that needed medical attention immediately. Her breathing was struggled and labored, and Erin could tell that she was in serious trouble. Erin had neither the medical equipment nor the time needed to save this poor girls life, but bent down close to see what she could do and was filled with sorrow as she saw that the girl had sustained what could only be a fatal injury. She could see that the girl's eyes were fixed and dilated, which was a sure sign of a brain injury. She glanced around the dark room looking for something in which she could use to stop the bleeding when Bobby motioned her away with his hand. Uncertain what she could do to help the child she hesitantly obeyed him. He had after all saved her life, and she was anxious to see what if anything he could do to help this girl. Tears leaked out of the young girls eyes, and shallow moans escaped her lungs, but the girl was not conscious. There was an ever-increasing pool of blood around the girl's head as it streamed from her wound, nose, and ears. Erin didn't know how the girl was hanging on, and didn't expect her to do so for much longer. And as Erin made room for Bobby next to the child, she decided that she had never felt so helpless.

Bobby placed his hands upon the girl's bloody forehead and scalp, and as if in response to his touch she began to convulse mildly. After a moment the convulsing stopped, as did the girls bleeding, and breathing.

Erin stifled the tears that were swelling behind her eyes, and swallowed the lump that had grown in her throat as she placed her hand on Bobby's shoulder. "I am sorry Bobby. We have done everything that we can," she said to him as she tried to pull him away from the girl, but he would not go.

"Come on Bobby," she said as she tried once again to pull him away, though stumbled back with shock when she saw the girl begin blinking her eyes.

"Holy mother in heaven!" Erin gasped joyfully as the girl began to sit up with Bobby's help.

"It is okay Sarah," Bobby quietly said to the young girl. "You are going to be okay."

Sarah sat up and looked at them questionably. "Who are you? What happened?"

Erin smiled as she helped Sarah to her feet while looking over her wound that was no longer there. "He had done it." Erin thought to herself. "I'm not crazy."

"Don' take my baby!" Screamed the girl's mother from under a pile of rubble. "Please don't take my baby from me!"

They had not seen the girl's mother, as she was in a dark corner half buried under a mound of debris, and probably unconscious. Now Sarah's mom was pleading with them not to take her child. Erin was shocked as she looked around in disbelief at the remnants of the destroyed house, that anyone had lived through this at all.

"There's another one! Another one is alive!" Erin shouted as she began to make her way to Sarah's mother.

"No!" Bobby yelled. "There will be others coming for her. We must go now."

"We can't just leave her like this!" Erin said as she again started towards Sarah's mother.

Bobby reached up and took hold of Erin's arm as she passed, and that was when all hell broke loose inside of her mind. It was as if Erin was somehow in Sarah's head, and she saw the horror and torment in which this innocent child lived. Sarah's memories became her own, and in so doing she became aware of the physical, psychological, and sexual abuse that this poor girl had endured at the hands of her parents, and she recoiled in terror.

As Bobby let go of her arm Erin swayed a little, and Sarah was there to give her support. When she looked back at the girl's mom she no longer saw a mother, but a human monster. The woman was impure and unclean, and for reasons that she could not comprehend, she feared her. She no longer wished to help this woman as she reeked of vileness and evil. Erin hesitantly turned away and started out of the room. She had never walked away from a person in need before. It went against everything that she believed in, and though as much as she hated herself for doing it, she knew that this woman deserved no help.

"Mommy?" Sarah said urgently as tears began to leak from her eyes. She was unsure who these people were that had helped her, but she felt connected to then somehow, and knew that she should trust them, that she should go with them. Though for all of the pain she had endured it was almost unbearable for her to leave her mother the way she was.

"Mommy!" Sarah said again as her leaky eyes turned into a river and she turned to run back to her mother in fear.

"Don't leave me baby!" Sarah's mother cried. "Come here baby, mommy will make it all better. Come on honey."

"No," Bobby said quietly as he took Sarah by the hand, and her eyes seemed to glaze over as her tears subsided and a small smile creased her lips. "We have to hurry, it may already be too late for some," he said seriously.

Sarah sniffled up her emotions, shook her head okay, and let Bobby walk her away.

Erin watched as Sarah fled back to her mother, and she was about to go after her when Bobby grabbed her hand. She watched carefully as Sarah said okay, and did what Bobby asked of her, the same way that Erin had. She knew that Bobby had done something to her; he had shown something to her with his touch. Erin wondered if the truth as told by Bobby was as hard for Sarah to accept as it was for her.

Bobby was puzzling to Erin, an enigma. He was different and special, of that she was certain, and his differences were subtle yet profound. He reminded her of one of those autistic children that she had read about, who had little to say, but who's eyes held a keen knowledge of things that were inexplicable to most. Bobby was not autistic, that she could clearly see, but he did seem to have that keen knowledge that most people lacked. His eyes appeared wiser than his years, and she feared him, just a little.

"No! Please no!" Sarah's mother screamed as they walked away. "Help me! Oh god no! Help me!"

Erin could not help but look back at the poor woman who deserved what she got. She felt a pang of remorse for leaving the woman to die alone, but could not bring herself to help her. Though as she looked back she began to wonder if the shadows and light were playing tricks on her eyes, or if she was simply losing her mind. For what she was seeing caused her skin to ripple with goose flesh and her heart skip a beat. She could hardly see the woman through the shadows, as the shadows themselves seemed to move over her like dark blankets. Erin then realized that the woman was no longer calling after her daughter, but calling for help as the shadow creatures preyed upon her.

"They are here!" Bobby screamed. "Come on! Come on! Hurry!" He shouted as he ran as fast as he could while pulling Sarah along.

Erin looked around with wonder and fear as she saw that all of the shadows around them seemed to be alive and moving. They came from every dark corner and deep crevice moving silently towards the helpless woman. Erin wanted to run but could not tear her eyes away from the horrible sight in front of her. Finally Erin broke away from her stare as the woman let out one last blood-chilling scream as the formless bodies of the shadows shifted and slithered upon her with dark intent.

She quickly caught up with Bobby and Sarah as they fled through the shattered house. She could somehow sense the evil that had taken place in this home, and it disturbed her deeply, leaving a bad taste in her mouth, and an ache in her heart. She wanted out of this house as bad as Bobby, and ushered them to go faster as they headed for the open door. On their way out Erin again saw the family photos that lay scattered on the floor, and could not help but to step on then on her way out.

They all rushed through the door, down the four-step porch, and out into the biting rain. The wind ripped at them savagely, but was very much welcome compared to the terrifying ordeal that they had witnessed inside of the house.

Erin was livid. She had absolutely no idea of what was going on, other than the obvious. But there seemed to be things happening beyond the veil of her understanding, and she knew that this unique little boy held the answers. Bobby was no ordinary child, that she could accept, but the manor and circumstances in which her reality was changing left her feeling impotent and fearing for her sanity. Bobby appeared to have known what those shadow creatures were, and seemed to be expecting them. Erin on the other hand felt as if she was left at Bobby's mercy, as he knew things that she did not. All of her medical training and field experience was ineffectual when compared to his healing touch, and she began to question her role in this horrible scenario. She was frightened, bewildered, and her emotions were tainted with feelings of inadequacy and meagerness. She felt as if she was losing control over the situation, the children, and herself, which made her feeling insubstantial and angry. She was after all the adult here, and did not feel comfortable being led by a six year old boy, no matter how special he appeared to be. With this in mind she decided to take back the authority and control in which she believed she had lost.

The three of them ran for shelter underneath a large overgrown box elder tree that grew next to the street in the front yard of Sarah's house. Erin stayed behind Bobby as they ran, and when they reached the tree she yanked him up by the collar of his shirt and held him against the tree's trunk.

"All right young man! Enough is enough!" Erin shouted at him, though it did not sound like a shout under the howling of the wind and drumming of the rain. "What's going on Bobby?" She demanded to know.

Bobby shrugged his shoulders shyly with fear in his eyes, all of the while trying to avoid her gaze.

"Don't give me that bullshit! Erin snapped at him as she jerked him roughly by his shirt collar. "What were those things in there? And how did you heal Sarah? And me for that matter?"

"I didn't," Bobby said as he shook his head with tears in his eyes.

"Don't lie to me! Don't tell me you didn't! I saw what you did in there dam it! This is important!" she said as she began to shake him.

Sarah stood by Erin's side and put her hand onto her shoulder. "Please. Please don't hurt him," she said fearfully and then cringed as she awaited Erin's response.

Erin then saw herself reflected in Sarah's eyes and thought of the horrible woman in which they had just left inside of the house, Sarah's mother, and she let go of Bobby's shirt. When she looked back to Bobby she found him crying and shivering, and she shook her head sadly as she began to cry herself.

"I am sorry," she said painfully as she took Bobby into her arms and hugged him tightly. She then pulled Sarah close and hugged her as well, and was pleasantly surprised and pleased when the girl hugged her back cautiously.

Erin's tears showed little of the pain and inner turmoil that was driving her at this moment. She felt as if she was on the edge of some bottomless chasm, her heels digging into the ground as she slides helplessly towards its gaping maw. She was losing it, she knew, as hard as she fought against it, she was about to go over the edge, over the edge of the empathy and compassion in which she had dedicated her life. Over the edge of all she had believed herself to be, and into the depths of the fear that had captured her, into the dark abyss of insanity. It was Sarah's eyes that had led her back from this dark place. It was the fear and uncertainty in them that gave her hope, and lent her purpose.

"I am sorry," Erin admitted shamefully. "I am just scared and confused. I didn't mean to take it out on you Bobby." Erin was sorry, and more fearful now than ever that she was losing control. She had always been a person who thrived in the face of adversity, and blossomed to her full potential when under pressure. Though today she felt as if she was falling apart, and even though she loathed to admit it, she knew that it was true. She held onto the children as if her life depended on it, and knew that she could not allow herself to go to pieces if for no other reason than the fact that these kids needed her, and she felt that on some level she needed them also.

She briefly wondered if perhaps she had suffered some kind of brain injury in the accident. Although she felt fine, she knew that severe head trauma would account for her confusion, anxiety, hallucinations, and any irrational thinking. It suddenly occurred to her that she could be in a coma right now, and all of this was part of some terrible yet fantastic dream that her subconscious had come up with to occupy her mind, though she knew that it wasn't.

The wind gusted strongly, blowing the cold rain at them with stinging force. They scrunched together and huddled next to the tree trunk, using it as a shield, and it helped somewhat. The air was chilly for early summer, and even though the days had grown long again the land looked shadowed and dim as a constant appearance of dusk shown in the skies.

Erin got down onto one knee to face Bobby at his level. She looked him straight in the eyes and tried to smile as he returned her gaze. "Did you see the shadows in there Bobby? Did you see them move?" She asked hopefully.

Bobby looked up to Sarah, and then back to Erin. He wasn't crying anymore, though the fearful look in his eyes remained. "Yes," he acknowledged with a shake from his head.

"I saw them too!" Sarah added. "It was scary."

"Yes it was," Erin said as she looked back to Bobby. She was pleased that she was finally beginning to get some answers, and hoped that the rest of her questions would be answered just as easily. She took his hand into hers, and was thankful when nothing unusual happened.

"What were they Bobby? What were those shadows?" she asked.

Bobby looked as if he did not want to say. He shuffled his feet as he looked to Sarah, who was also waiting for an answer, and then stared off towards the sky.

"Please Bobby," Erin urged. "I need to know. I need to know that I am not going crazy."

Bobby looked into her eyes and smiled sadly. "It was the Sentinel."

"What is the Sentinel?" Erin asked as Sarah leaned in closer to hear over the wind.

"They are a force of nature, like we are," he said simply enough as if it was nothing out of the ordinary.

Erin looked to Sarah, who shrugged her shoulders, and then again to Bobby. "Why are they here? What do they want?"

Erin thought that Bobby was about to answer when they were distracted by a shrill whining sound that reminded her of the slow creaking of an old door with a rusty hinge, though one thousand times louder. They all turned back towards Sarah's house and watched as the building began to shudder. There were earsplitting snapping sounds that Erin guessed were the support beams giving way, and then the structure collapsed with a sound like dynamite detonating, and the house crashed to the ground. An immense plume of dust and smoke lifted up into the rainy air as flames immediately sprung up from the rubble. A powerful explosion ensued, and three of them fled out of the yard and into the street.

They stood in awe as they watched Sarah's house as it became engulfed in flames.

Sarah stood next to Erin watching in horror as everything that she had ever know came toppling to the ground. Everything and everyone that she had ever loved as well hated lay trapped in the inferno in front of her, and she wasn't quite sure how to feel, though the tears in her eyes seemed appropriate. Bad things had indeed happened in that house, terrible things in which she would never forget, and part of her was happy to see it burn to the ground. Yet there were also good times that were equally unforgettable, and she closed her eyes against the tears as she remembered them. She was an only child, and therefore all of her parent's attention had been focused on her, both good and bad. Her birthday parties had been extravagant with clowns and inflatable jumping gyms. She had always gotten the best presents, everything that she had asked for, always. She *was* loved, she knew that, though her parents had also done things to her that she could not understand, and although she knew it was wrong, she let them because she loved them too. Her parents, no matter how bad they might have been, were still her parents, and she already missed them. She found solace in Bobby's touch as he somehow sensed the melancholy emotions that were plaguing her mind and took her hand and held it tightly.

Sarah felt connected to Bobby in a way like she had never felt with anyone before. She was comforted by the mere touch of his hand, and although her future was an ominous black hole in front of her, his touch was soothing and welcome. And even though she couldn't see past the life in which she had lived thus far, and she knew that things would never be the same, Bobby's eyes told her that everything was going to be better than she had ever imagined, and it was that thought that carried her through as she watched her past, both good and bad, as it was consumed by fire.

Erin decided that the questions could wait until they found a safe place to wait out the storm, and began looking for a house in which they could find shelter. Most of the houses on the left side of the street (the side on which Sarah's was) had been nearly destroyed, or severely damaged by the tornado, while the houses on the right side appeared to have suffered no heavy damage, in fact some of them appeared untouched. She took up one of both Bobby's and Sarah's hands, and began to lead them towards one of the houses that had been unscathed by the twister.

"No!" Bobby yelled as he tried to pull his hand out of Erin's grip. "We have to go! Now! My mommy will be waiting! She will be scared. She needs me!"

Erin shook her head. "No Bobby! It is just too dangerous right now," she said as she pointed towards the tornado that could still be seen in the distance. "I promised you that I would help you find your mother, and I will. But your mom would want you to be safe first and foremost; you have to trust me on this. As soon as the storm is over we will! I promise you!"

"No!" Bobby shrieked again. "I can't be late. It will be too late!" He then stopped walking and continued trying to pull away.

Erin could understand how scared this kid was, she was after all terrified herself, but as the only adult here it was her responsibility to get the children out of harms way. She already had too much weighing on her conscience, and was not about to let either of these two kids get hurt, or worse. The truth about Bobby's healing powers, and of the strange shadow people could wait, as could Bobby's mother. They needed shelter above all, that was their main objective at the moment. Weather Bobby agreed with it or not was of no consequence to her right now. She was a paramedic, and had dealt with irrational people more than once, and she tried to believe that this was no different. She had a job to do.

Sarah stopped while Bobby and Erin debated on which way they should go. She was alone now, and it really didn't matter to her where they went. She found a strange sense of peace in that knowledge, as if anything was possible, though the tears continued to leak from her eyes. And although her eyes were flooded, they were also opened to all of the possibilities that life had to offer. It was Bobby that had freed her, this she knew, and she would follow him wherever he went. In Bobby she found a ray of hope that had been long forgotten and sorely missed. Bobby and Erin was now the closest thing she had to a family, and she did not want to see them argue. She was about to say so when she heard a noise from above, looked up, and screamed.

Sara's scream caught both Erin and Bobby's attention. Simultaneously they followed Sarah's eyes and looked skyward. A thin funnel cloud was spiraling out of the clouds overhead, stretching towards them. The sound it made was terribly sickening and sounded like a chorus of screams as it reached down towards the earth.

5

Todd shuddered as the horrific winds unhinged the cellar doors and sent them spiraling up into the tornado. He clung fearfully to the house's old water pipes while the fierce winds spun through the cellar threatening to pull him free from his grasp on the plumbing. Struggling with all of the might that he could muster he strained to maintain his grip, though he feared that it would not be enough. Above he could hear the tornado as it ripped and tore through the house, and he waited to see if the ceiling could support the disaster that was taking place above him.

With grinding teeth and watery eyes he tried not to think about his present struggle, and thought instead about Erin. Never in his life had felt so guilty about anything as he did for leaving her after the crash. Although he knew that with the twister so close behind them there had not been any time to think or second-guess himself. He had reacted with his own best interests in mind, thinking solely of self-preservation, and even though that might have been the right choice, hell, the only reasonable choice, it still left him feeling contrite and culpable. He had let her down, and now it was too late to do anything but what he had come here to do, save himself. He knew of course, that the crash had most likely killed her. From what he had seen it had been a bad one, and neither of them had been wearing their safety belts. If he had been wearing his seat belt he knew that he would not have been thrown from the vehicle, and right now he wasn't so sure if that had been a bad thing.

Todd could remember leaning out of the ambulance window to get a good look at the tornado that they had spotted. That was when Erin bore down on the accelerator, picked up speed, and ultimately lost control. His eyes were focused on the twister behind them, and he could not rightly remember what it was exactly that had caused the ambulance to crash. Erin had been skillfully trained with years of driving experience behind her, and he was sure that whatever it had been was beyond her control. Todd could recall being launched from the ambulance and onto the pavement, and he winced a little at the memory. He could not remember actually hitting the pavement, but he remembered rolling to a stop with the tornado only one or two short blocks away. Bruised, bleeding, and badly shaken he hobbled away as fast as he could go, though he regrettably had no time in which to save Erin. And even as the memories surfaced and he knew that he had made the only choice he could, he still could not forgive himself for not trying.

He had found this cellar lust moments ago, and it was within mere seconds after that the tornado had come upon him.

He had run to the nearest house in sight, which was right next to the school in which they had crashed in front of. He ran to the small one story house as fast as his battered body would allow, even though it was directly in the path of the oncoming tornado. With time running out he banged on the doors and tried to shake them open, but the house was locked up tightly and seemingly deserted. Quickly he started moving around the house thinking to try the back door. That was when he had noticed the cellar, and decided to take cover there. The cellar wasn't locked, and he slipped inside just as the winds rose up and began to excel.

Now, as he sat in the darkness of the basement cellar he prayed that Erin had somehow survived the crash, and made it out of the ambulance before the tornado hit. Hope and prayer was all that he had to hang on to now as he imagined the tornado spinning directly over him. The foundation of the house began to shake and tremble, and somewhere in the back of his mind he thought that the whole house might be uprooted as in the Wizard Of Oz, though he could not imagine a fanciful world of munchkins awaiting him inside of the tunnel above.

The water pipe that he had been holding onto began to shake wildly, and then began to leak, soaking him with a cold spray. At that same moment all of the cellar windows simultaneously burst inwards sending a shower of glass raining down upon him. Much of the glass was caught up in the ferocious winds that blew through the cellar with such tremendous force that it propelled each fragment of glass as if shot from a gun. Todd tried to shield his face from the sharp projectiles, though he could feel them stick into his flesh with stinging pain. The water pipe finally gave way, and was wrenched out of his hands and sucked up through the ceiling. "This is it! This is the end." Todd thought as the wind caught him along the flank of his body knocking the wind out of him, and sent him sprawling across the hard concrete floor. The gale flowing through the basement was pulling him towards the cellar entrance, and though caught in its grip, he scrambled to find something to hold onto, some perch in which he could anchor his life. With a scream caught in his throat he flailed for something, anything, and at last his hand caught hold of another, smaller pipe only five feet from the stairs and doorway. He held onto this pipe with everything that he had and then some. One of his shoes came off as he kicked against the wind and was sucked out of the cellar and up into the screaming vortex. The screaming sound of tornado was merely the howling of the wind accelerated and amplified hundreds of times, though in his mind he thought he heard voices, not voices exactly, but screams directed at him, telling him to let go, to join them in the chaos above. At this he found his voice and added his screams to the chorus. He screamed to drown out the voices in the wind, in his head, or wherever they were coming from. He had no intentions of letting go, and did not want to hear any encouragement to the contrary.

Todd was beginning to think that this tornado was going to last forever, as it already seemed to him like hours since it had hit. He knew that in reality it had probably only been seconds or minutes, but he supposed that time would seem to stretch when you were as terrified as he was. Time fly's when your having fun, was the old cliché, and if that were true, than he supposed that the less fun you were having, the slower time would seem to go. In any case, he was eager for the tornado to pass.

He pulled himself close to the small pipe and looped his arms around it snugly. The wind appeared to be slowing, though it was no less threatening as he could still feel it's grip as it tried to bring him free from the pipe. Knowing that the tornado was moving away made him feel a little better, but he then got a whiff of natural gas that made his stomach tighten into a knot. He looked over the pipe in which he had been holding on to, and heard a small hiss coming from it.

"Oh shit!" Todd said as he looked towards the cellar entrance, and then again at the pipe. This would be just my luck, he said to himself. I survive being thrown from the ambulance window, and live through a hellish tornado only to be blown up while hugging a gas pipe, just great. The wind continued to die down, and at last he felt safe enough to let go of the pipe. Getting to his feet he inched towards the doorway and saw that the tornado had indeed passed. He climbed a couple of the steps leading out of the cellar and peered out into the gloomy day beyond. The tornado was now over the school, and as he looked for the ambulance he climbed up another of the stairs. It was gone, the whole damn thing was gone, and his heart sank. There was destruction everywhere, and he sadly surmised that there was no way that Erin could have escaped both the crash and the tornado. Climbing the last few steps that led out of the cellar he turned and looked at the house that he had taken shelter underneath. It was gone as well. Nothing remained of the small house except for rubble and debris. Todd was in awe of the horrific power of the twister, and stood amazed as he surveyed all of the damage it had done thus far. Though, it was not over yet, as he could still see the cone shaped spiral as it made it's way deeper into the small town, and he was unsure of what he should do next. There would be lots of people, who were going to need help, but right now the streets were deserted and he was unsure of where to start.

Turning away from the cellar and the remains of the house, he started towards the light pole in which the ambulance had ultimately crashed into. The pole itself no longer stood erect, but was bent and twisted with its peak resting upon the ground. Wincing in pain, he began pulling out the fragments of glass that had been imbedded in him as he walked. They were many and numerous, with much of them in places that he could not reach. He stopped to pull out a particularly troublesome piece of shrapnel when he heard a crash coming from the rubble of the house behind him in which he had taken refuge. Turning around he expected to see the remainder of the house collapse into the cellar, but was surprised to see a man emerge from under a collapsed wall. He was bloody and staggering, and Todd ran to him.

Ignoring his own pains, cuts, and bruises, Todd leaped and jumped over the debris to reach the battered man. He was now wearing only one shoe and he tried to be careful not to step on anything sharp or pointy as he went, though he cut and scoured his foot more than once on the glass and nails that jutted up from the debris. As he made his way Todd saw the man fall down with a scream, and he hurried even faster and more recklessly.

Todd didn't know what he was going to be able to do without his medical equipment, but he did know that it was often the simple things that saved lives. He had been trained for just this sort of emergency, and although he had years of experience, and had confidence in his skill, he nevertheless felt nervous and unprepared.

When he did finally reach the patient, he found that the man had not fallen down, but was kneeling over the motionless body of his wife.

"My name is Todd. I am an Emergency Medical Technician from Harvard," he explained as he went to work. "What is her name?" He then asked as he checked her airway, pulse, and circulation.

"Cindy!" Said the man. "Is she? She's not dead is she?" He asked fearful of what the answer might be.

"Cindy? Cindy! Can you hear me?" Todd asked after finding that she was breathing, and did have a pulse. Cindy did not respond. "What is your name sir?" He then inquired.

"Brad," said the man. "Is she going to be okay?"

Todd shrugged his shoulders and shook his head. "I don't know yet. She is alive, but she is in shock. We are going to need some blankets."

"Blankets?" Brad asked as he looked around in wonder at the remnants of his home.

"Yes! Blankets, towels, clothes, or anything else that you can find to keep her warm," Todd said urgently. "And we are going to need something flat that we can carry her out of here on. There is a gas leak."

"Okay," Brad said as he shook his head and darted off into the rubble in search of the items that Todd had requested.

Todd then quickly assessed Cindy's injuries. First he noted a large goose egg bruise on her forehead that was more than likely a concussion and the reason for her unconsciousness. He found several broken ribs, and suspected that she may have some internal injuries. Checking her eyes, he found that her pupils were equal and reactive to light, which was a good sign.

At this point Brad returned with an armful of wet blankets, clothes, and linen, and then without a word went in search of something flat and large enough in which they could use to carry her on. Paying little attention to Brad, he rechecked her breathing and pulse. Her pulse was rapid, but strong. Her breathing was labored and heavy, and on closer inspection he heard a gurgle in her breath that gave him concern, though he concluded that though unconscious, she was stable for the moment.

Brad returned dragging behind him the top slab of his dining room table, and he laid it down next to Cindy. "How is she doc?"

Todd looked up to Brad and noticed how badly he needed medical attention also. He had a visible gash on the front of his scalp that was bleeding badly, and many other cuts and puncture wounds around his body that if were not controlled quickly enough would surely bleed him to death. But Brad seemed okay for the moment, and his first thought was to stabilize Cindy, and get them away from the house, and out of danger.

Todd nodded approvingly. "I can't be certain, but for the moment at least, I think she will be all right. She needs more help than I can give her here, but for now." As he spoke to Brad he wrapped the wet clothing around her neck as a make shift cervical collar to keep her neck immobilized, and then instructed Brad on how to best move her onto the table for transport. Then ever so carefully they rolled her onto the table, and preceded to cover her with the other material Brad had found.

Together Brad and Todd Carried Cindy through and out of the rubble, and deep into the back yard safely away from the house and the gas leak. They set her down carefully, and Todd found a fallen limb in which to place under the table at Cindy's feet to keep them elevated, and her blood pressure up.

Todd then looked to Brad, who was growing paler by the minute, and decided it was his turn to be treated. "Come here Brad," he said. "Let's get you taken care of too."

"Don't worry about me," Brad suggested. "Just take care of Cindy. I will be fine."

Todd shook his head. "No you wont! Listen, I might need some help here, and you're it! And you aren't going to be any good to me, or to Cindy for that matter if you pass out from losing too much blood. Now get over here."

Brad shook his head, and then reluctantly knelt down next to Todd and allowed him to treat the most severe of his wounds.

"Okay," Brad said begrudgingly. "Just please don't let Cindy die."

"I will do everything that I can," Todd assured as he began ripping one of the shirts that Brad had found for Cindy. He tore the fabric into long strips in which he used as make shift bandages and tourniquets. As he bandaged Brad's wounds he noticed that this guy was as tough as nails, and appeared to feel no pain at all. Brad had sustained many injuries; though most were minor puncture wounds and lacerations. There were however a couple of injuries that needed immediate medical attention. One was a sever laceration on his forehead, that would not stop bleeding, and Todd fashioned a bandana out of the torn shirt and tied it around his scalp. The other was a huge sliver that had penetrated his chest. Todd quickly pulled out the two inch long piece of wood, and quickly bandaged the wound without so much of a flinch from Brad. Todd then bandaged up a few other wounds that Brad was bleeding through.

"All finished," Todd said as he completed applying the Bandages, and then looked down to Cindy, whose condition had not changed.

Brad sat close to her and ran his bloody fingers through her beautiful hair while leaving streaks of crimson in her golden locks.

Brad looked to be about forty years old, with dark hair and a short beard. His wife Cindy looked years younger than him, and had soft blond hair and an hourglass figure. Todd could see why he loved this woman, and that caused his thoughts to turn to Erin, who had just reciprocated his affection this afternoon, and was now probably dead.

Todd took a moment to investigate his own injuries and found none too severe. He had a nasty abrasion from his spill on the roadway that ran down the length of his body. It burned like fire and ice, though was not serious of life threatening. There were still many pieces of glass embedded in his skin, but they were mostly concentrated on his back and were beyond his reach. His shoeless foot was bleeding and sore, and he decided not to remove his sock, as it was the only protection that his foot had. He then began pulling out the little bits of glass that was within his reach when he was distracted by a loud creaking sound. Glancing to Brad he then stood up and looked around in search of the source of the eerie whine.

"What the hell is that?" Brad asked as he too was trying to figure out where the sound was coming from.

Todd shrugged his shoulders as the creaking stopped, and a loud crash ensued. Brad jumped to his feet and stood next to Todd as they watched a cloud of dust and smoke rise from the other side of what was left of the school.

"Holy shit! What was that?" Brad asked.

Todd was about to say that he didn't know when whatever it was exploded.

6

Bobby broke into a run as he noticed the funnel cloud stretching towards the ground. His short legs quickly carried him back across the street in front of the houses that had already been damaged by the first tornado. He paid no attention to either Sarah or Erin as they followed him, calling his name.

"Bobby!" Erin shouted as she ran after him as much as she was running from the tornado. He ignored her as he had done earlier, and left her guessing as to what he was thinking. She no longer cared if he was special, or if she was crazy, all that she wanted to do was to get these children out of danger, but to do that she would first have to catch the boy. Finding a place to wait out the storm should be his first concern, though he seemed to be on some kind of mission that was going to get them all killed.

Erin didn't have to turn around to know that the funnel cloud had touched the ground, as she could hear it's thundering presence close behind. She pushed herself as hard as she could as she struggled to catch up with Bobby and Sarah, who were both a short distance ahead of her, with Bobby in the lead.

Sarah was in a daze. She wasn't at all sure about what had and was happening, though she knew that Bobby was the answer to her unasked question. She felt drawn to him in a way that she didn't understand, yet at the same time somehow made sense. There was something about the way he had touched her that made her feel clean and pure again. The affect brought back a long lost sense of innocence and hope, and she wanted that. Needed that. She called his name as she ran after him, though he did not turn or stop, and she then did not turn or stop as Erin called after her. She did not want to lose sight of Bobby for fear that she would lose him forever, and she already felt as if she had lost more today than she cared to. Erin was slowly catching up to her, and for that she was grateful, for she liked Erin, who had showed to her a warm sense of kindness that had touched her deeply in the short time that had been together. Erin was not far behind her now, and the tornado not nearly far enough away.

She followed Bobby's path along the street, and though she kept her eyes focused on him she saw something out of the corner of her eye that chilled her far more than the weather. Her heart was pounding and cold rain and sweat streaked into her eyes blurring her vision. She squinted her eyes and wiped at them with the palm of her hand hoping that what she had seen was a product of her imagination, though when her eyes had been cleaned of the sweat she only saw them more clearly. She saw the shadow people. She saw them peek and hide, moving from shadow to shadow like whispery patches of dark mist. They seemed to appear and disappear like magic, their sleek transparent bodies just one shade darker than the dreary day. There were a lot of them. Sentinels, Bobby had called them. They were as quick as lightning and almost invisible, but she saw them. They were following Bobby also.

Erin caught up to Sarah, and together they chased after Bobby. He was nearly fifty yards ahead of them and showed no signs of slowing down. He had run past Sarah's demolished house, and now continued down the street. After passing four houses he slipped in between the fourth and fifth, and disappeared into the back yards.

"Bobby!" Sarah screamed as Erin took up her hand to help her along. Though upon seeing Bobby disappear between the houses she got a burst of adrenalin and sprinted out in front of Erin.

They ran past the houses and into the back yards where Bobby had gone, though he was still out of sight. Behind the houses in the back yards it looked like a war zone, as downed trees, lawn furniture, and pieces of aluminum siding and roofing tiles laid everywhere. Erin's heart sank when she could not find Bobby, and

Sarah stopped in front of her as they both searched frantically for any sign that could tell them which way he had gone. They didn't have time to stop and try to figure out in which direction he had gone, they had to guess quickly and hope for the best. Picking the easiest route, Erin once again snatched up Sarah's hand and began leading her through the yard, though it had been the wrong direction and Bobby appeared, showing them the way.

"Come on!" They heard Bobby demand as he appeared from behind a fallen Elm tree, and then disappeared once again.

The chase continued as Erin and Sarah both looked back and saw that the tornado was still behind them. It was gathering force and speed, growing larger every second. Erin didn't think that anyone could be lucky enough to live through two tornados in one day, though she really hadn't expected to live through the first one. She knew that she was pressing her luck, and would not have bet on her odds of making it out of this alive.

They quickly followed Bobby as he ran through the back yards, away from the school. He had lost some of his lead by stopping for them, but he still had a twenty-yard head start, and Sarah and Erin struggled to close the gap between them. They were catching up to him. He was fast, but they had a fear of the tornado that Bobby did not share.

Bobby continued running without looking back. He appeared to be following the same path as the first tornado, and then as he emerged out of the yards and onto an adjoining street he changed directions and deviated from the original tornado's path. He ran down the street a short bit, and then ran towards the houses across that street, and into those back yards. There was a set of elevated railroad tracks behind the houses at the far end of the yards, and Bobby ran towards them oblivious of the tornado that was consuming everything behind them.

Erin was right behind Bobby. She was almost close enough to grab a hold of him. Sarah was running beside him, though she did not try to stop or slow him down. There was a drainage ditch that ran lengthwise along the tracks, and was filled with water. As Bobby stepped down he misjudged its depth and fell hard, splashing into the muddy water. He then turned around and Erin saw his eyes fill with wonder as he gazed up to the enormous tornado that was nearly on top of them.

Without hesitation Erin jumped into the watery ditch, grabbing hold of Bobby as she landed. Sarah then grabbed Erin's shirtsleeve and began shaking her as she glanced back to the nearing tornado. She could see the tornado bearing down on them out of the corner of her eye, and frantically searched around them for someplace to hide. Almost directly in front of them was a drainage pipe that went under the railroad tracks. It was roughly four feet wide, and she barely noticed it behind the tangle of weeds that had overgrown its entrance. Big enough for them, Erin decided. It appeared to be choked off at the other end, as she could not see daylight through it on the other side.

Erin held Bobby by the loop of his pants and pushed him towards, and into the large pipe. He struggled, though not much, and was ushered inside by Sarah who eagerly followed. Erin then scrunched in after them, pushing them until they were in the middle of the concrete tube. It was a tight fit, and the pipe was one quarter filled with cold water, but they made it inside before the tornado hit.

"Brace your legs against the pipe!" Erin screamed to be heard over the tornado that was already making its way onto the railroad tracks.

Bobby, fearless as he was, tried to crawl over Sarah and Erin to get out of the pipe, though the girls held him back.

"No Bobby!" Erin yelled as she grabbed hold of him, and held his upper body in a giant hug, and Sarah did the same with his legs. Together Erin and Sarah held him as tightly as they could, while bracing their legs against the powerful force of the twister.

The tornado hit furiously causing Sarah and Erin to scream with fear. All of the water was sucked out of the pipe and up into the tornado. Sensing their fear Bobby stopped struggling and let them hold him, and he in turn held onto them.

The wind and water tore at them viciously as the full force of the tornado came upon them. The sound was deafening as well as terrifying, and they found it hard to brace themselves with their muscles shivering with fear. Debris slammed against the opening of the pipe with terrible force as they struggled under the intense vacuum that the tornado created inside of their shelter.

Sarah could feel the pull of the tornado trying to dislodge her from her brace against the pipe, and she knew that she would not be able to sustain her position under the immense pressure of the twister. Bits and pieces of earth and roots were torn free from the clogged side of the pipe, stinging her face and arms as they were sucked out. She struggled to maintain, though she could feel herself slipping, and finally had to let go of Bobby. She then pushed against the pipe wall with her hands as well as her legs, screaming as she did so. Still, it was not enough and her legs gave out, sending her slamming up against Bobby and Erin.

Erin struggled with all of her might to keep hold of Bobby, while also keeping Sarah lodged behind them, though it was a losing battle, and she screamed as her feet began slipping across the smooth surface of the pipe. She applied every last ounce of strength that she had, fighting against the pull of the tornado, though she knew that it would not be enough, and tears began to leak from her eyes.

Sarah had a moment in which to reposition herself after her legs gave out, and while lodged snug against Erin she once again braced her legs against the piping, held onto Bobby, and strained against the powerful beckoning wind. Just as she had herself positioned correctly she began to feel Erin slowly slipping away and she screamed to her.

"No! Erin, hold on!" she cried as she relinquished one of her arms from Bobby, and grabbed hold of Erin's wrist. "Hold on!" she screamed again as she gave Erin a pleading glance just before her feet slipped. And then it was over.

As quickly as the tornado had come, it had also gone, over the railroad tracks, leaving them shaken and sore. The wind had died down, and the air pressure seemed to return to normal, though Sarah continued to cling to Erin's wrist and Bobby's legs.

"Let me go!" Bobby demanded as he began kicking and wiggling wildly to get free.

Sarah then realized that she was still hold onto Bobby and Erin with a death grip that was bringing her used up muscles close to a cramp. She let go of Bobby, and then slowly let Erin's hand loose.

Erin and Sarah lay at the bottom of the concrete pipe as it slowly began to fill up with water again. Her heart was pounding, and her hands, arms, and legs were trembling. Bobby was crawling over them to reach the pipe's exit, and Erin reached up and grabbed his ankle.

"No Bobby!" she said somewhat out of breath. "Please don't."

"I have to," Bobby said with a sad smile. "There isn't much time! We have to hurry before it is too late. My mommy, my daddy, they need me! Please! You said that you were going to help me," he pleaded with her.

Erin did remember saying something like that, but she had thought that she was dying at the time, and she didn't know that she would be risking their lives while fulfilling her obligation. She felt sorry for Bobby. She didn't know who he was or what he had been through, but he was nearly hysterical now, and her heart went out to him.

She shook her head. "We aren't going to be able to help anyone if we don't take care of ourselves first Bobby. I know that may sound callus, but it's true," she said sympathetically. "We have to be smart about this."

As Bobby continued to try to pull away Erin propped herself up on her knees and took hold of his wrist before letting go of his ankle. Using his strength as he pulled away from her she got to her feet. The tornado was now fifty yards away from the railroad tracks, and though it was quickly moving away from them the wind and rain were fierce nonetheless.

Sarah cautiously crawled out of the drainage pipe, as Bobby continued to try and break free from Erin's grip. Erin was entranced by the tornado as she stared at it in wonder as it continued to bore a path of devastation through the neighborhood. She had beaten the odds and cheated death three times today, four times, if she included the flash flood in which she and Todd had nearly gotten stuck. Then as she turned away from the twister she noticed the vague unnatural shadows creeping towards them. She gasped, her heart skipped a beat, and Bobby broke free from her hold.

"Bobby!" Erin tried to scream, but her voice was caught deep in her throat as he stomach tightened in fear of the Sentinels as they approached. Their nearly transparent figures shifted and glided effortlessly through the ominous light of the storm. They moved like liquid smoke, and Erin saw their fiery eyes as they moved towards her.

Bobby splashed through the water and scaled the small rise on which the railroad tracks had been set. There was an intense look in his eyes that made him look old as he glanced back at them, and then continued over the tracks.

"Erin!" Sarah screamed fearfully from on top of the tracks as she motioned for her to follow. "Hurry!"

Erin broke free from the grip of fear that held her and looked up to Sarah. Bobby was already over the tracks and out of sight, presumably chasing after the tornado. She scrambled up to the tracks, and once again followed Bobby as he ran ahead.

It only took a few moments for Erin and Sarah to catch up to Bobby, though this time Erin had no intention of trying to stop him. The shadow people were right behind them and gaining fast.

She didn't know what these Sentinels were, but Bobby seemed to know, and he was running.

The tornado was only a block ahead now, but appeared to be moving away from them faster than they were running towards it. Deadly debris that had been picked up and then discarded by the twister rained down all around them. Some of the debris was as small as a marble, while other pieces were larger than she was and could cause substantial bodily injury, though she feared the Sentinels more, and did not look for cover. She could not see the shadow people now while she was running, and was afraid to look back in fear that they might be there, closer than before. They ran through the wreckage of houses, cars, and past things that were no longer recognizable. The destruction that the tornado left behind was total and complete, though consumed with fear, Erin hardly noticed as she ran.

They emerged out onto a street that Erin recognized. It was State Line Road, the road that separated Wisconsin and Illinois. It was also the border of the town of Sharon. Ahead of them laid vast fields of corn, on mostly flat farmland. Uprooted, ears of corn flew past them like pieces of shrapnel as the tornado ripped through the crops.

Erin and Sarah expected Bobby to follow the twister through the crops, but he stopped upon seeing the flashing lights of a police cruiser, and started running towards it.

Finally, Erin thought to herself, Bobby is being sensible, and looking to the police for help. Though as they got closer she noticed that the police car had crashed into a light pole at a T shaped intersection, and the dark figure of a body lay in the street about one hundred feet in front of the disabled police car.

Bobby saw the body of the man in the street, he was a police officer, and he ran to him. He pushed himself as fast as his short legs would allow. Ignoring the pain and exhaustion, he fought against the breakdown that he felt so close to. "It wont be long now," he told himself as he tried harder to run faster. "I am almost there mommy!" he said to her as if she could hear him.

As Bobby reached the body in the street, he tried not to turn away. The officer's face was ground almost to the bone. Bits of flesh and muscle clung to his skull, and his eyes stared sightlessly towards the dark sky, fixed open, as he no longer had any eyelids. Three of the four of his limbs were twisted in unimaginable ways, wrenched and twisted with sharp bone protruding from more than one limb. There was blood, but not much as the tornado and rain had washed it away, and Bobby feared that he might not have been fast enough.

Bobby held his arms back to prevent Sarah and Erin from getting too close, as they almost ran into him.

"Stay back!" Bobby demanded as he knelt down next to the broken and crooked body of the town Sheriff, who's nametag read Michael Hershey.

Erin had been a paramedic for a long time, though she had never seen such a gruesome sight, and from the way that Sarah recoiled she knew that it troubled her as well. Still, they watched closely as Bobby knelt down next to the shattered body of the officer waiting to see what he would do.

Bobby reached out and prepared to place his hands upon the officer's body when the policeman woke up with a start and growled viciously. With a snarl he cocked his head, and looked at Bobby wickedly.

Sarah screamed when the disfigured corpse came alive, which made Erin jump, leaving her unprepared when Bobby leapt back from the body as it reached for him with its one good limb.

Erin was caught completely off guard as the carcass came to life, surprising her and Bobby, who fell back into her, knocking them both down while Sarah screamed.

"**You can't have them all Bobby!!**" the corps growled violently in a voice that reminded Erin of an old exorcism movie she had once seen.

"**The rest are mine!!**" it hissed malevolently with vile contempt as it continued to reach for Bobby. It's one good hand clawed at the air in front of them, while it's other useless limbs writhed and squirmed upon the ground, making awful cracking and grinding sounds as it's broken bones scraped against one another. Its sightless, hollow eyes stared them down with an intensity and hunger that was palatable.

Erin watched in horror as she got up and helped Bobby to his feet. Sarah had stopped screaming, though she covered her mouth with her hand as if she was holding it back.

"Stay back Sentinel!" Bobby ordered. "You are not needed here!" he said as movement caught his attention up ahead. The policeman in the car had slumped over the steering wheel causing the horn of the car to sound.

Erin watched as Bobby dashed around the writhing body of the sheriff and sprinted towards the disabled police cruiser. Carefully and quickly he evaded the officer's grasping fingers, and once he had past, the policeman's body went limp and slack as whatever had possessed him relinquished control. Then in horror she took hold of Sarah's hand and stepped back as she saw the shadow people, the Sentinel, leaving the corps of sheriff Michael Hershey. There were many shadows seeping from the crumpled body, and they were right behind Bobby, chasing him, or racing him Erin thought. She hadn't seen any fear in Bobby's eyes, and she began to wonder if this wasn't some kind of horrible competition. And if it was she feared to guess what prize was at stake, though she knew that this was not a game.

"Go Bobby! Run!" Sarah screamed to him, fearful of what would happen if the shadow creatures caught up to him.

Holding Sarah by the hand, Erin cautiously led her around the now lifeless corpse and began jogging towards the police car and after Bobby.

It was neck and neck, as Bobby appeared to be running on top of the shadows. They were almost to the car, and Bobby began screaming as he ran. He sprinted the last few steps, and as he reached the car he dove through the drivers side window and into the car. At the same time the shadow people seeped into the vehicle through every crack and fissure until they could no longer be seen, and the persistent horn ceased.

Erin cringed as she watched Bobby dive head first into the window and through the glass that shattered around him. She squeezed Sarah's hand tighter as she heard the girl gasp, and they hurried their pace. Worried for Bobby's safety they plunged ahead unsure and unconcerned about whatever dangers the Sentinel might pose. Bobby had risked everything so that he could help them, complete strangers, and although they were afraid and uncertain, they could do no less for him.

Bobby opened the door to the patrol car and slowly crawled out. Blood saturated his clothing and was dripping down his face and arms. He looked pale, tired, and was gasping for breath. He looked up to Erin and Sarah as they made their way towards him and tried to get to his feet, but his muscles failed him and he slipped helplessly back onto the concrete.

Erin stopped in her tracks as Bobby hit the pavement. She wasn't far from him, but did not want to lead Sarah into a situation in which she had no understanding or control. She didn't know if it was the glass or the Sentinels that had caused these injuries to the boy, and told Sarah to wait behind while she moved ahead. Sarah nodded without saying a word; but her eyes showed how terrified she was even though her expressionless face was slack with fear. Erin ran to Bobby, this, she thought, this was what she had been training for. All of her medical schooling and experience had been for this moment. She hoped that it would be enough.

As she reached Bobby he raised his weary bloodied face. He pulled himself up onto his side, still breathing hard, and tried to smile.

"Are you okay?" Erin asked as she immediately began to examine him to determine his injuries. "Where are you hurt? Lie back down now," she said as she cradled him in her arms.

Bobby smiled. "I am fine. Just tired is all." He then wiped his bloody hand on his jeans and scooted himself into a sitting position.

"But," Erin said. "All of this blood? Where…?"

"Jack," he said as he pointed to the policeman in the car. "It's jack's"

Erin looked into the car and then back to the boy. She wiped the blood away and found that he did not have any apparent wounds. She shook her head as she gave him a close hug as Sarah came over to join them, still fearful that Bobby was hurt.

"He is all right," Erin told Sarah with a sense of relief. She then looked into his eyes and saw that he was exhausted. The day's events had certainly taken their toll on him and it showed. He had been pushing himself so hard, too hard. He was after all just a boy, not a Navy Seal or Green Beret. He was special, that was for sure, yet he was still just a six-year-old child, a child that held too much on his shoulders, and pushed himself too hard. She could see that his expectations of himself were unrealistic, though everything about him was unreal, surreal, and vague. She didn't know what he was capable of, and therefore did not know what to do for him. She did know that she could no longer stand in his way. Something was happening here in this small town, something extraordinary, and it was as horrifying as much as it was fantastic and amazing.

"He is going to need you, he will be confused" Bobby said as he got to his feet while the officer began to cough and gag inside of the car. "Help him and then follow me!"

"Okay," Erin reluctantly agreed with a shake of her head, and then watched as he ran towards the side street and the distant tornado. He ran through the grass, past a street sign, and then down the road. As she looked after him the street sign caught her eye, and what she read sent shivers down her spine. The sign read Burr Oak road. It was the street in which her and Todd had been trying to reach, and she was reminded of the poor elderly woman who was in the midst of a heart attack. Her sympathy went out to the old woman who was undoubtedly still waiting for her arrival, though there was nothing that she could do for her now, and Erin began to feel helpless and small.

"I am going to go with him," Sarah said as she took her hand out of Erin's and slowly started walking away.

"No," Erin pleaded. "I think you should wait for me." But Sarah had already turned around and was jogging away.

"I have to." Erin heard her say as she followed Bobby down the street. Erin was about to go after her when the officer's coughing stopped, and she turned towards the man. He was coming awake and she started to go to him but stopped when she saw the shadow people as they began to ooze out of the car like some kind of dark liquid. She stepped back unsure of what was going to happen, though was surprised when they fled right past as if she were invisible, and within a moment they were gone.

"Are you all right in there?" Erin asked as she took a step towards the car. The policeman had stopped moving, and as she drew closer she half expected the deputy to sit up and try to grab her as the sheriff had done to Bobby. "Hello?" she called. "Can you hear me?" There was no response, and she moved closer still. She was close enough to touch him now, and against her better judgment she reached in to tap him on the shoulder.

His hand was quicker than her eye and in that instant he reached up and took hold of her wrist. She screamed as she yanked her arm out of his grasp, stepped back and waited for the low guttural demonic voice that the sheriff had used just moments ago, though it did not come.

The deputy's eyes fluttered open as he glanced around him seemingly unsure of where he was. She suddenly realized that she was alone, and felt vulnerable and frightened. She wished that Sarah had stayed with her, though as she looked down the road she found that Sarah was already out of sight.

"Holy shit!" the deputy said as he jumped in his seat, looking frightened and thoughtful at the same time. "What happened? Is it over?"

"Yes," Erin said with a sigh of relief, glad to see that he was not possessed as the sheriff had been. "No. I mean the tornado is still on the ground," she explained as she pointed to the top of the twister that could still be seen over the tree tops a couple of miles away.

"Wow," said the deputy as he squinted his eyes to see the tornado more clearly. He then gasped as he noticed all of the blood that had painted the dashboard and windshield red. His clothes were soaked with it, and he quickly checked himself over to make sure that he was uninjured, and then looked to Erin. "Who are you?" he asked. "How come I am still alive?"

Erin didn't have the answer to his second question, and was not about to tell him the truth, whatever that was. She didn't have time for explanations even if she had one. She didn't know what was going on here, though she did know that she wanted to be a part of it, and *it* was all about Bobby, and she was anxious to get moving again.

"Listen, deputy Blake," she said as she read the nametag that he wore on his chest. "I am a paramedic from Harvard."

"John," the deputy casually said as he cut her off. "John Blake, but you can call me Jack. Everybody else does."

"Okay, Jack," she said, trying to be patient. Though she was eager to be on her way after Bobby and Sarah. "Two children have just run down Burr Oak road here, and are chasing after the tornado. I have to stop them, and I am going to need your help."

Jack nodded as he tried the ignition key and was disappointed when nothing happened. He then got out of the car and looked to Erin, who was already inching her way towards the street.

"We have to hurry!" she said as she looked down the street, and then back to Jack. She was sure that it had been a mistake to let Bobby and Sarah out of her sight, and now her fear grew with every passing second.

Jack was a strong man, of both mind and body, and he struggled to rationalize what had happened. Something had definitely happened here, as the blood soaked car interior was a sure sign, but logic eluded him. He knew that he should be dead, but was unscathed, and then he noticed the disfigured corps of his partner lying in the street.

"Oh no!" Jack said as he went to him, and then Erin was there, pulling him away.

"No!" Erin said sympathetically as she took his arm and turned to face him. "There is nothing you can do for him. I am sorry, but there are two kids that desperately need our help. Please, you have to trust me." She gave him a pleading glance, and then turned and started down the road after the children.

Jack looked back to the motionless body of his old friend Mike, and then to the ground. Even at this distance he could see the twisted position in which his partner laid, and knew that it was hopeless. He was a cop above all, and knew that he must go where he was needed. Pushing his feelings and emotions to the back of his mind he looked down the road and followed after Erin.

7

Todd and Brad glanced at each other as they heard the explosion, and each of them took a step closer to get a better look.

"What the hell was that?" Brad asked as he gazed over the school at the rising dust and smoke.

Todd shrugged his shoulders. "I don't know. Maybe another gas leak."

"Maybe," Brad said as he looked at what was left of his home, and then down to Cindy who remained unconscious. "Do you think that we're far enough away?"

"I think that we are probably safe here," Todd assured him, and they both looked back over the school. Flames could now be seen through the hazy smoke licking up towards the sky, and then like a nightmare another tornado formed, reaching out of the heavens towards the earth.

"Oh my god!" Todd said uneasily as the twister spiraled out of the heavy churning clouds, and touched the ground on the other side of the school. His first thought was to pick up Cindy and run, though on further inspection he noticed that the tornado was moving away from them, following the same path that the first one had. His heart was pounding rapidly, and he could feel a nervous sweat beading on his already wet forehead. With a lump in his throat he searched the sky all around them for any signs of another tornado, but was relieved when he saw none. For now at least, they were safe.

"I have never seen anything like this!" Brad gasped as he observed the tornado with a glassy look in his eyes. He too gazed up to the sky expecting to see another twister bearing down on them from another direction, and was also set at ease when he did not see one. He then knelt down next to Cindy and picked up her hand as she began to moan painfully.

"Cindy! Honey, it's Brad," he said as she opened her eyes and looked up at him.

"It hurts!" she said quietly as she bit her lip, straining to endure the pain that was so obvious in her eyes.

Todd bent down to check Cindy's pulse again, and found that her heartbeat was still strong and steady, though rapid.

"Who are you?" Cindy asked Todd as she began to cough, and a bloody froth spewed from her mouth and nose. She then tried to scream out in pain, though she could not seem to find enough air, and it came out with a garbled gargle.

"What's wrong doc? What's happening to her?" Brad asked as he began to panic upon seeing the blood.

"Try not to talk Cindy. My name is Todd, and I am an Emergency Medical Technician. We are going to help you, all right?"

Cindy shook her head with fear in her eyes, though said nothing as she spat the blood from her mouth and it rolled down her chin.

"It is going to be okay honey. You are going to be fine," Brad said as he tried to assure her, and reassure himself, as he did not want her to see how worried he actually was.

"Cindy," Todd said, interrupting Brad as he tried to sooth his wife. "Can you point to where it hurts for me?"

Cindy nodded as she brought her hand up, and pointed to her head.

"Okay Cindy, anyplace else?" Todd asked, although he thought that he already knew what the problem was. And when she pointed to her chest she confirmed his suspicions. "Okay, now just try to relax."

"What is it?" Brad asked. "She is going to be okay, isn't she?"

"She needs to get to a hospital," Todd began, but was then cut off as Brad snapped at him bitterly.

"No shit! We all need that! Just tell me if she is going to be all right! All right?" Brad said fearing the worst.

Todd ignored Brad and spoke to Cindy, who lay there painfully waiting to hear how bad it was. The pressure in her chest was excruciating, and there was dizziness swimming through her head that made her feel nauseous. She placed her free hand over Brad's and listened as Todd explained to them the details of her injuries.

"It could be worse," Todd said. "Aside from the concussion you received, I believe that you have several broken ribs. I am pretty sure that one of these fractures has punctured one of your lungs. This would explain the blood. But you are stable for now. Still, I think that if we can't get you to the hospital immediately, we should at least get you out of this weather, to someplace safe." He then looked to Brad, who shook his head in agreement.

"I will find us a way to the hospital," Brad declared to Cindy as he stood up, and began running out of the yard, looking for a house that had not been ravaged by the tornado.

Todd sat next to Cindy, and held her hand softly as he continued to watch the skies. He could not see the twister anymore, as it had moved away quickly, and was shielded by the trees. He then looked down to Cindy, and wiped away the tears that were streaming out of her eyes.

"Todd," Cindy whispered painfully. "Am I really going to be okay?"

Todd shook his head. Yes, I think so. I am sure that Brad will find you a way out of here."

She tried to smile, but then began coughing once more, as she continued to lose blood.

Todd was afraid that she would soon drown in her own blood if a chest tube was not inserted quickly enough. She was stable for now, but he had seen conditions such as hers before, and he knew how quickly things could change. He silently prayed that Brad would be successful, and would not be too long.

Brad ran as fast as his sore and bruised body could go. His, was the only house on this side of the school, and he would have to travel another block to find a house that had not been severely damaged by the twisters. He ran past the school, and as he did he saw that Todd's ambulance had been thrown through one of the school walls. He thought about going to the rescue vehicle and trying to use it's radio to call for help, but did not want to waste time on something that probably wouldn't work, and kept running.

He came to the street on which he had seen the second tornado develop, and saw that it had been the old Collins place that had exploded and gone up in flames. He felt bad for them, as they were nice people, and he hoped that they had all made it out in time. Most of the houses on that block were left in a state of devastation, and he past that street and continued ahead. Further down the road he was on were five houses, three of them on the left, and two of them on the right. He went to the left, to an old couple's house that he had never met. Sharon was a small town, and everybody seemed to know everybody, though the old couple that lived here didn't get out much, and Brad had never met them. It was a charming little two-story cottage, with wood trim, a shag roof, and a well-manicured lawn.

As he ran up the walkway he noticed a plaque stating that this was the Spino residence, and under that plaque was another that read, never mind the dog, beware of the owner.

Ignoring the warning Brad leaped onto the porch and began pounding on the door. "Please help me!" Brad pleaded to whoever might be listening on the other side of the door. "My wife is dying! Please answer!" He tried the doorknob and found it locked, and then continued to pound on the door.

"Hey! Is everything all right over there?" The neighbor from across the street hollered.

Brad spun around and saw that it was Kip. He was sitting on the tailgate of a truck with his friend Danny. They were a couple of young guys who he had drank a few beers with a couple of times. They were even now holding beer cans as they sat there under the drizzle.

"Is that you Brad?" Kip asked as he stood up from the tailgate.

Brad turned away from the door and ran across the street. He went as fast as he could go and slipped on a patch of gravel in the road, and then righted himself in an almost graceful stumble.

"Holy shit Brad! What happened to you?" Danny asked as he slid off of the tailgate and stood next to Kip as they watched him scramble across the lawn.

"Can't you see that my fucking house is gone?" Brad asked angrily as he bent over trying to catch his breath. Though as he looked towards his house he noticed that he could see little of anything through the tall shrubbery and short trees that lined the driveway.

Kip shook his head. "What? We just came out. The television isn't working, but the radio said that there were tornado's spotted around here. So we are, well, tornado watching."

Brad shook his head as he stood up. "Well you fucking missed them. But I didn't. Look man, it's Cindy, she's hurt really bad! I need a ride to the hospital. She might die!" He put his hands on Kips shoulders and shook him gently to express his urgency. "Can you drive us? Please! I need your help."

"I will drive you!" Danny announced with a look of fear and hope, and then ran inside to retrieve his keys.

"Are you all right Brad?" Kip asked genuinely concerned. "You don't look so hot yourself."

"Yeah," Brad said as he tried to catch his breath. "There is some hippie paramedic with Cindy now, and well, he patched me up a bit too."

"A hippie paramedic?" Kip asked with a queer grin.

"Yeah, not much of a driver though, he parked his ambulance inside of a classroom at the school."

"No shit?" Kip asked.

Brad did not answer, as he saw Danny run from the house towards the old primer gray Chevy pick-up truck that he was driving these days.

Brad's house could not be seen from the driveway due to the thick bushes, and Kip ran down the length of the drive to the edge of the street to get a look. He stood in horror seeing that not only was Brad's home leveled, but so was half of the school. He saw smoke spiraling up into the sky, but could not tell exactly where it was coming from. A knot tightened in his abdomen as he realized how easily it could have been his house, and them, who were living this tragedy, and the enormity of the situation came crashing down upon him. Swallowing hard as a lump grew in his throat, he tossed his beer can aside and wished that he had not drank so much today. Brad and Danny had gotten into the truck and were backing out, and as they passed Kip he jumped into the back of the truck.

Danny squealed the tires as he pulled out of the driveway. He slowed down a little when he saw that Kip was jumping into the bed of the truck, but he didn't slow much, and he flinched when Kip hit the back window with his shoulder.

As they backed onto the road Brad looked over to the Spino residence and saw that someone was holding the curtains back, looking out of the window. He wondered if the extra minutes that it had taken him to find a ride would ultimately cost Cindy her life, and as they began to drive away he gave the peeper the finger.

***

Todd let go of Cindy's hand. He was beginning to wonder what was taking Brad so long. It seemed like he had been gone a long time, and he was beginning to worry over Cindy's condition. He stood up and stretched his sore legs, looking for any sign that Brad might be coming, though he saw none. He looked down to Cindy, she was fading, it was slow, but he could see it. She needed surgery as soon as possible, sooner than possible under these circumstances, and from the look in her eyes he suspected that she knew this also.

"Where's your partner?" Cindy whispered to him clearly.

"What?" Todd asked, although he had heard her question clear enough. Erin had stayed in the forefront of his thoughts throughout all that had happened, and he did not want to speculate on where she might be now.

"Your partner?" Cindy repeated. "Don't you medical people always have a partner?" she asked.

"Yeah, I have a partner," Todd said as he knelt down next to her again. He picked up her hand, and noticed that it was as cold as ice, and had very little strength. "As soon as you get on your way to the hospital I am going to find her," he said as he fought against the tears that were hiding behind his watery eyes. "I am going to find her, and anyone else that is hurt."

"Were you close? What happened?" she asked.

Todd did not want to talk about this right now, and was pleased when he saw the pick-up truck approach. "Brad's back with a truck!" he told Cindy with a smile, though a tear leaked from his eye, and he quickly wiped it away.

"Oh good," she said quietly as though she were very tired.

Todd got to his feet as he waited. He saw that the truck would not be able to make it all of the way to them through the wreckage of Brad's house and took a couple of steps closer as he watched them park in the front yard.

"He brought help too!" he relayed to Cindy excitedly, as he saw two young looking fellows following Brad as he ran across the yard.

"Cindy?" Todd said loudly after she failed to answer. He looked back and saw that Cindy's eyes were closed and she was as motionless as a rock. "Cindy!" He yelled as he went to her. He knelt beside her and took up her hand as he shook her.

"Cindy! Can you hear me? Cindy?" he called to her.

"I can hear you!" Cindy snapped at him. "It just hurts to talk," she said with grinding teeth.

Todd sighed with relief as Cindy snapped at him, and he could not help but laugh, just a little bit. She in turn started laughing also, and then winced in pain as her chest contracted.

"Oh shit!" Cindy complained as she began another series of messy, bloody coughs.

"Sorry," Todd said to her as Brad and his companions arrived. They came bounding over the rubble like warriors, and Todd was filled with passion, as he was warrior also. He had survived, and because of him, hopefully many more would survive.

"How is she doc?" Brad asked as he reached them at a dead run.

"I am fine," Cindy said coarsely.

"We are going to get you to the hospital dear," he said as he picked up her hand as Kip and Danny picked up the makeshift stretcher and began moving her towards the truck. "You are going to be fine baby," he consoled her, though the fear, worry and hope was apparent in his voice.

Danny and Kip slowly carried her over the rubble towards the waiting pick-up truck as Todd trailed behind. He had done everything that he could here, and was anxious to find Erin. He was holding onto a vague shred of hope that she had survived, and like he had, found shelter someplace, in the nick of time. He had to make sure that she was all right, or god forbid, dead somewhere. He loved her. He knew that now, and although he did not expect a miracle, he silently hoped and prayed for one.

"Nice park job with the ambulance," said one of Brad's friends as he laid the top of the makeshift stretcher in the bed of the truck, and helped slide it in the rest of the way.

Todd gasped. "What do you mean? Where is she? Where is it?" he questioned.

Brad could see the concern in Todd's eyes, and answered for Kip, who was not paying attention enough to reply. "It is in the school." He said solemnly, suddenly aware of what he might find there.

"Inside of the school?" Todd said with a ghostly expression on his face. "I have to go now! You guys will be fine. Just get her to the hospital and you will be fine."

"Thanks Todd, for everything," Brad said as Todd turned without answering and ran quickly through the debris towards the school.

8

Cliff carried the candle through the dining room and into the living room. His heart was heavy, and his mind numb with fear for Ruby. She was dying. He was sure of it. It had been more than forty minutes since she had called for help, and now the phones were dead. Her condition had not changed, and against his better judgment she insisted on drinking more wine. He carried her wine glass in the opposite hand of the candle, and set them both down on the coffee table in front of her.

"Thank you Cliff," Ruby said as she picked up the wine glass with a trembling hand and drank deeply.

"You're welcome dear. There isn't any more though. That was the last of it," he explained as he sat down next to her and placed his arm around her shoulders pulling her close. "I think there is some brandy way back in the pantry if you have to have something," he said.

"No, I think this will be quite enough. I am fine," she told him as she placed her glass (half empty) back upon the table. She then picked up his hand and kissed it warmly. She smiled as she looked into his old, tired green eyes. He was a beautiful man, the kindest man that she had ever known. Sure, he wasn't much to look at these days, but then neither was she, and besides, she saw beyond the flesh to what was important, she saw what nobody else could see, and she knew that she was lucky to have him.

"Oh, you old fool!" Ruby said as she reached for a kiss.

Cliff obliged and welcomed her touch, and when she was done he continued to hold her close and returned her kiss with another, longer, deeper one.

"How did you ever end up with such a woman as me?" she asked as she placed her head upon his chest.

"Just lucky I guess," said Cliff as he tried to hide the tears that had begun trickling out of his eyes. "Just plain stupid luck. You deserve better than me."

"Bite your tongue!" she snapped back at him as she adjusted herself to give another kiss, and then noticed his puffy eyes and wet cheeks. "Are you? Oh Cliff, please don't, don't cry."

Cliff bit his lip instead of his tongue as he fought against the emotion that was building up inside of him. He could see that she was in pain even though she tried to ignore and conceal it, and he did not want to upset her any more than she already was. Though when she saw the tears falling from his weathered eyes he could see her face change, and her beautiful hazel colored eyes swelled with moisture, and began to leak also.

Cliff watched as her tears broke free as if they had been silently building, just waiting for a chance to escape, and when they came, they came in a flood. And Cliff was then powerless to hold back his own emotions that were swelling inside of him.

The storm raged on outside. Inside they cried, holding each other. They heard the strong gusts of wind as their home moaned and creaked as it strained against the weather, but it was now forgotten in the midst of their pain. The rain came and went, drumming loudly on the roof of their trailer. The thunder crashed and echoed as the lightning struck, but the storm was no longer any of their concern, and had been all but forgotten.

Ruby could feel her heart begin to stagger, and even though it frightened her and caused her to become dizzy she remained strong.

"I love you Cliff," she said as though it would be her last time saying those words. "So, so much!" she said as she clung to him, finding comfort in his arms.

" I love you too Ruby. More than you could ever know," Cliff announced proudly. "I will always love you, and there will never be another that I could care for more," he said as the dam within him broke free, and although he had been crying, his tears now rushed forth with such emotion that he sobbed like a child, and buried his face into Ruby's soft hair.

"Please stop Cliff," Ruby urged as she stifled her own tears. "There will be plenty of time for tears. Let's not squander whatever time we have. Let's be happy for now, together, you and me. Why don't you go and find that bottle of brandy, and get a glass for yourself while you're at it," she said and then turned away as if he had already gone to do what she had asked. She looked out of the large window at the storm, and as she did she felt as if the storm she saw was raging inside of her. The thunder rumbled as her muscles shivered and twitched with pain and fear. The lightning struck igniting the heavens causing her heart to tremble and palpate at irregular intervals. The wind blew feverishly causing her to become dizzy and faint. Still she struggled against it, trying to will her anxiety away, burying her fear and pain for Cliff's sake.

Cliff tightened his grip on Ruby as she turned away, and for a moment he just sat there holding her, not wanting to let her go, afraid of what might happen if he did. He felt things too deeply, loved her too much to just turn off his emotions and get the brandy. He was bound to her in some metaphysical way that defied boundaries and defined love, and he could not bring himself to leave her. "No honey. No more." Is all that he could bring himself to say as he choked the words through his sobs.

130

"Please," Ruby said as fresh tears found their way down her cheeks.

Cliff shook his head. "Oh Ruby," he began, though the words were caught in his throat and barely audible.

Ruby turned and wrapped her arms around him. She hugged him as tightly as she could as she too continued to cry. "Listen dear, I am seventy-nine years old!" She said almost ruthlessly, though with a smile. "And I would like some brandy. I do not need to ask you if I can have it, or even if I should. So get off your lazy ass, and do this one last thing for me!" she snapped with an unbridled vigor that Cliff did not expect, and then gave him a sweet kiss to let him know that she was being spontaneously playful.

Cliff was shocked by her fresh kiss and put off attitude under these conditions, but he knew her well, and could sense a game when he saw one. She may be dying, but she was not dead, and Cliff did not want her to die in fear. This game seemed to be her last wish, and although he was reluctant, he decided to let her have it.

"Listen damn it! I am your husband and I will decide what you can or cannot have, and you are not having any brandy! And that is all there is to it. Understand?" Cliff asked through the lump in his throat. "Besides, you know darn well that it is my brandy, and you are not allowed."

Cliff heard her snicker as he let her go, got up, and slowly walked to the pantry. He was still crying, as he knew that this would most likely be their last time playing this game, and any other for that matter. He glanced back as he walked through the dining room and into the kitchen and saw that Ruby was indeed snickering, though it was through her tears and his heart went out to her. It was good to see her smile in the midst of this horrible moment. She was a strong woman, and he knew that it had been her who held him together through all of the rough patches in his life, and though he knew that it was a selfish thought, he could not help wondering what would become of him without her. It was her strength of spirit that empowered him, her charismatic approach to life that inspired him, it was the thought of making her smile that lent fulfillment to his life. Her unwavering faith and enthusiasm taught him new things every day, and as they grew old together he had realized how much more there was to know and learn from this dear woman he loved. Though he could not find a lesson in today's events, he was sure that there was one, and was equally certain that Ruby would point it out if asked. He would not. This would be a lesson that he would have to decipher all on his own. A lesson he would only have to learn once. A lesson he did not want to learn.

"You wouldn't even have that brandy if I hadn't gotten it for you Cliffy," Ruby said in an accusingly playful tone. "So I think you might bring me some anyway, you think?"

"Don't count on it!" Cliff hollered as he searched through their overstocked pantry. He was not a drinking man by nature. It caused him to lose control, and he feared that more than anything, and he realized now how out of control he really was, in the greater scheme of things anyway. Sometimes though, when the moon was full, he welcomed the invigorating presence of alcohol in his system. It had a way of warming him all the way to his soul, and his mind opened up to new possibilities. Occasionally he liked to drink a bit (always a bit, nothing more) while he was reading fictional stories, as he seemed to envision things more clearly, and could lose himself in the pages more easily. He also drank when they played the games that they would sometimes play, games like the one they were playing now. Sometimes sex was difficult at his age, at to keep things fresh and interesting they would sometimes play games, games of arousal. They had even been known to fake a fight now and then just so that they could make up afterwards. This was different though, and he found it hard to keep his attention focused, and he knew that there would be no arousal.

He found the nearly full bottle of brandy and then retrieved a wine glass to match Ruby's. He stopped half way through the dark kitchen and set the bottle on the counter top. He tried with little success to hide his sorrowed feelings. Picking up a dishcloth he said a silent prayer as he dried his eyes.

Dear god, you must know that I have always tried to be here for you, to be a good person. I am not by any means perfect, but I try. And if you were ever going to give me anything else before I died, please grant me this; keep Ruby safe at home with me.

"What are you doing in there Cliffy? Ruby called from the living room. "You know, you are going to drive me to drink."

"Coming dear," Cliff called out as he picked up the bottle and looked to the ceiling as if he could see heaven from his kitchen. *"Please lord, just one more hour, one more day. Please!"* he whispered, and then went to Ruby.

"Well, it's about time," Ruby said with a smile, though she knew that she could not hide her discomfort completely. "I was beginning to think that I was going to have to find another bar tender," she said almost cheerfully.

Cliff could see how hard it was for her to keep up her smile, and decided that he did not want to play this game any more. He did not want a drink, and could not keep his worry hidden behind a false smile.

"Ruby," he pleaded. "You do not have to do this. Not for my sake. We could just sit here and wait for the ambulance. I am sure that they will be here any minute."

Ruby looked up to Cliff through her watery eyes and let her smile fade. She could feel her bottom lip begin to quiver, and she reached for Cliff's hand. "Oh Cliff! I am so scared!" she said as he came to her.

"I am right here baby," he said as he set down the bottle and glass and sat next to her. He wiped the tears from her eyes and then kissed her moist cheek. He found her trembling as he put his arm around her, and kissed her again on her forehead. "Oh honey, I am right here."

Ruby held on to Cliff with every once of strength and energy that she had. She had never been so frightened in all of her life. She knew that this moment came to everyone at one time in their lives, though she found that a whole life of preparing for death was not enough, and she was terrified. Her chest felt as tight as ever, as if there was someone standing on top of her, and then jumping up and down. She began gasping for breath as she pulled her arms away from Cliff and gripped her chest fearfully as she began to grow dizzy. As she did this she saw the horror in Cliff's swollen eyes, and was scared for him too.

Cliff heard the storm outside swell, and their trailer home began to tremble and rumble. He was considering taking a look outside when Ruby withdrew her arms and gripped her chest. She had a horrible look on her face as her eyes grew vacant, and he knew that god had not granted his request for more time with her. Not a day, not an hour, nor a minute. He was taking her home now.

"Ruby? Ruby!" Cliff exclaimed as he placed his hands on her lap helplessly. She was dying before his eyes, and he once again began to cry. "Oh my Ruby!" Cliff called fearfully as the storm continued to grow louder. She was trying to say something to him, and he hushed her, he knew what it was.

"I know Baby, I know. It's all right, I love you too." Cliff had to yell these words as the weather outside made it nearly impossible to hear inside their home. Though Cliff failed to notice the rising storm as his thoughts were with his wife. He took her by the shoulders and looked into her eyes wondering what he should and could do, though before he could do anything the front window exploded, sending a cold rain of glass over them.

Cliff instinctively shielded his wife with his body as the window shattered, and then hugged her closely to keep the blowing wind and rain from her face. He looked into her eyes and saw that she was still alive, but was hardly breathing. He briefly wondered if he should try CPR, or perhaps try to breath for her, or both. But as he began hearing the sounds of other windows shattering throughout the house he knew that shelter would have to be his first concern.

With his old age forgotten, Cliff picked Ruby up as if she were a child and carried her away from the window. He could feel the cold rain streaming in through where the window had been, and he absentmindedly thought he saw a tree blow by. He had never seen weather like this before, and the word *tornado* came into his mind. The trailer was shaking badly as he carried Ruby through the house towards the bathroom, which was the only room that did not have any windows in it. He could hear metal bending and things breaking as he went. The wind inside of the trailer grew to an unbelievable strength. He reached the bathroom and awkwardly carried Ruby through the doorway. Once inside Cliff carefully laid Ruby down in the tub and shut the door. He called her name, though he could not even hear himself as it sounded as if the trailer was being torn apart.

"Ruby!" Cliff hollered, and when she did not answer he began shaking her gently. "Ruby!" She did not answer, and he crawled into the tub with her, holding her tightly as he waited for whatever was coming next.

"Dear god!" Cliff cried as he once again looked up to the ceiling as if he could see god there. *"Don't leave me alone like this! Oh god please no!"*

This time Cliff's prayer did not go unanswered, and as he looked towards the ceiling it was torn away. He then saw the hand of god in the form of a merciful tornado as it picked them up and carried them away.

9

The rain had begun falling steadily once again as Erin glanced back, finding that officer Jack was jogging behind her trying to catch up. She tried to hurry after Bobby and Sarah who had a pretty good head start. She could see Sarah's vague outline ahead in the distance, but the boy was lost in the mist and raindrops that separated them. The tornado could be seen about a mile or so ahead and was a looming monster that stirred uneasy feelings inside of her. She was afraid of what Bobby might do if and when he caught up to the twister. He was a unique and special child, that much was obvious. He seemed to grasped things on a different level than others, a level unfathomable and nonexistent to most. Erin thought that she was beginning to understand him a little bit, but she was certain that whatever it was that made him special had it's limits, and she did not think that he stood a chance against a twister like the ominous one ahead. No one did.

"Wait up!" Jack pleaded as he struggled to reach her.

Erin looked back and shook her head. "I can't!" she yelled with what little breath she could muster. "I have to reach Bobby before he gets to the tornado!" she said, and pushed herself harder and went faster than she believed possible. Her muscles burned and threatened to give out, but she stayed strong and continued trying to push herself even harder.

Within a moment Jack had caught up with Erin and was slowly pulling ahead. He didn't know who bobby was, but would do everything within his power to help. He was just ahead of Erin and going as quickly as possible. At almost fifty years old he found himself running much faster than he thought he was able. His back seemed more flexible than it had in years, and was without the usual aches and pains that it normally would have had in a circumstance such as this. It then occurred to him that never in his life had he been in circumstance such as this.

Erin had been pushing herself too hard, and found her strength ebbing away as this rigorous pace began to take it's toll. She looked over to officer Jack. He looked fresh and invigorated as he pulled ahead of her. She could no longer see Sarah in the distance and fought to keep up. She saw Jack look over at her and slow down with her.

"No, keep going!" she called to him. "Save the children!" Jack nodded to her as she watched him pull ahead once more, and she noticed how well he could run at his age. She suspected that even out here in the boonies, a police officer had to be held up to some physical standard.

It was growing harder for Erin to catch her breath, and she feared that her asthma was returning. She tried to pace her breathing but found it hard to regain her rhythm, and then her feet went out from under her as she slipped on some loose gravel in the road. She landed solidly on the wet pavement as her soft flesh scraped across the roadway like wood against sandpaper. Oddly enough she felt no pain, but was certain that she would feel it later. She let out a struggled yell, and then rolled to a stop.

For just a moment she laid on the pavement trying to catch her breath. She gazed up to the cloudy sky as the stinging rain pelted her face. The cold rain felt good as her whole body burned from overexertion. Her breath returned quickly and she made herself sit up. She could see Jack speedily running after the children. He turned back to look at her and she motioned him ahead with a wave of her hand. Wearily getting to her feet she took a couple of deep breaths and continued on as quickly as possible. She slowly picked up her speed as she went, but did not push herself this time, as she did not want to risk another tumble that might put her out of this morbid race.

Jack felt bad for Erin, who had just taken a nasty spill on the pavement, but knew that she was not in any danger, at least for the moment. Though the way his day had been thus far he believed that anything could happen. The tornado loomed wickedly in the distance, and he could feel his stomach churn as he grew closer to it. It was immense and awesome, as it seemed to be growing larger before his eyes. It appeared to be hovering over the Points Of Light trailer park, which only housed a dozen or so trailers. He sadly wondered how it was that tornados could always seem to find a trailer park. As he grew closer still he spotted the girl. He didn't know her name, but called out to her uselessly as the thunder of the tornado drowned out all other sounds. She appeared to be calling after the boy, who he saw was walking frighteningly close to the twister.

"Oh no!" he said to himself as he ran faster yet. Debris was picked up and spat down by the tornado and rained down everywhere. It was a dreadful sight, and against his instincts and better judgment he ran unnervingly close to the twister towards the children.

10

Bobby stood at the edge of the tornado, his eyes wide with wonder. It was frightening, and yet at the same time beautiful. Standing at the threshold of such immense power made him feel small and vulnerable, and although he was terrified, he knew what he had to do. He could hear Sarah begging him to come back, though he couldn't, even though he wanted to more than anything. He belonged here; this was his destiny. His first steps into the twister were the hardest, and tears rolled down his pale cheeks leaving streaks dirt. This was something in which he knew that he could not walk away from, as frightened and unsure as he was. This was why he was here. He had saved a few worthy souls along his way, and now with the tornado looming frighteningly before him it was time to complete his journey. He knew that this was something that Erin, Sarah, and Jack could not understand, but he also knew that things would become abundantly clear to them soon enough. Starting forward he moved slowly, not looking back in fear that he would lose his nerve.

After the first couple of steps he picked up his pace, anxious to be done with this business. The wind was incredible and overpowering as he reached the wall of the ferocious vortex. His tears were pulled from his eyes and taken up into the twister, and then he was gone as well, drawn up into the cloud of debris.

11

As he ran on Jack watched in horror as the little boy stepped into the tornado and disappeared behind a helical of rain and deadly debris. Tears leaked out of his eyes, as he knew that he had not been fast enough, and being in the presence of such a monstrous tornado seemed to bring out emotions that were best kept buried until he had done what was required. He found that the twister lent him a sense of reality that he could only compare to the eye opening experience of the psychodelic drugs in which he had tried in his youth, and it frightened him. This was no hallucination, and there were lives at stake. Trying to ignore the strange feelings, sensations, and emotions that haunted him he summoned all of his strength in an attempt to reach the young girl before something happened to her. He considered trying to call out to her, but he was using each and every breath to keep himself going. She was screaming and crying at the tornado as if the boy might still be alive, and could possibly hear her. She was standing next to the trailer park's manager's office, which was also a home. It was a two-story brick building, and was the only structure left standing in the area. It's roof was gone completely, and several of the walls had given way and collapsed under the powerful force of the twister, though for the most part the home remained intact, yet it had the appearance of a house that had been gutted by fire, and looked deserted and unstable.

"Hey! Hey you! Stop!" Jack called out to the girl. She appeared to hear him as she glanced in his direction, and then ran into the old burned out looking building anyway.

"Damn it!" Jack cursed as he chased after her. He had hoped that finding the children would be easy, and it was, but he had thought that the kids would listen to him, or at the very least come to him for help. Instead they seemed preoccupied, and took little or no notice of him whatsoever, nor for their own safety. He began towards the house as she ran into it. The tornado was only a hundred or so yards away, and the old brick house laid in-between him and the twister. He was unsure if tornados ever went backwards the way it had come, and stayed suspiciously aware of what the tornado was doing, and where it was going.

Out of the corner of his eye Jack saw the impossible. He saw the boy. Unsure of what he was seeing Jack stopped and peered deeply into the tornado. Squinting his eyes he searched for any sign of the child, and then he saw it again, a vague outline of the child, and then it was gone once more. He shook his head, knowing that his eyes must be playing tricks on him, but continued to look anyway. He found that the child was gone, and he wondered if he was really ever there.

Jack spent a moment surveying the tornado, looking for the boy that he was sure he had seen, but he could no longer see anything but the twister and the cloud of debris it carried within. He thought of the strange psychodelic feelings he was having, and briefly wondered if this might be a dream. Though he didn't have to pinch himself to know he was awake, as the child's screams he heard coming from within the brick building would have awoken him instantly. It was the girl, and she was in trouble. Jack didn't think twice before racing towards the Points Of Light trailer park's manager's office, and after the one child in which he could still save.

12

Sarah pleaded with Bobby, but he would not listen. She was scared to death, and could not bring herself to come any closer to the gigantic twister that lay in front of her. She painfully watched as Bobby slowly walked up to the twister, almost as if he was contemplating it, and she screamed when he took those final fatal steps into the arms of the tornado. She wanted to be with him so badly that she almost ran after him, but she couldn't. She knew better.

Sarah was about to give up on Bobby. Her hopes and fears seemed as if they had become one, inseparable and identical. Tears streamed out of her tired eyes as she looked down. She felt beaten and defeated, alone in a cold world of uncertain tomorrows. Turning away from the tornado she looked up to the dark sky, wondering if there was indeed a god up there somewhere, and of what he must be thinking at this moment. It was then that she heard Bobby, or at least thought she heard him in the midst of the thunder. She turned back towards the tornado as he called to her again. This time she heard him more clearly. It was him! She smiled in spite of her tears and called back.

"Bobby? Is that you?" she whispered. When she heard him once more she realized that his voice was not coming from the tornado, but from the brick house that was the only thing to withstand the twisters onslaught. She was standing close to it, and although she could not rightly explain how Bobby was still alive, or how he had gotten into the decrepit looking house, she went to him eagerly. She wiped the tears from her cheeks as she ran. Her smile filled with hopes of joy and reunion. As she ran she saw the police officer that Bobby had healed. He was calling to her as he raced to catch up. She wondered if perhaps it had been the officer that she had heard calling, and had mistakenly thought it was Bobby, but then she heard him again.

"Sarah! I need you Sarah!" the voice pleaded. "I need your help! Please!"

Sarah did not give it a second thought and sped towards the house to see what she could do for Bobby. With the officer and the tornado all but forgotten she reached the old wooden porch that led to the main entrance and stopped in front of the four stairs that led up to the wooden platform of the small deck. In the strange light of the storm the rust colored brick of the old house along with the collapsed side of the building made the house appear as an old ruin that had lasted the test of time. She could imagine, as she looked around the bleak landscape; that this could be the ancient dwelling of a civilization long since gone.

The sky was darker than ever, as the tornado blocked the dim light that did penetrate the clouds, and all was left in a sullen gray that was devoid of color. She could feel her heartbeat begin to quicken as she started up the porch steps and deeper into the shadows. The railing that had once enclosed the porch was gone, and only shards of the boards managed to stay attached to the wooden platform. They stuck up like spikes and daggers along the deck's edge, and left her with a creepy feeling that chilled her deep within her soul. She began to shiver as her wet clothes and the chill inside left her cold. The wooden steps creaked under her feet and sounded oddly loud compared to the tornado that loomed behind her.

She began to have second thoughts about going into this place and looked back to officer Jack. He was slowly catching up, and she wondered if she should wait for him. She began to wonder if she had really heard Bobby at all. She had after all been through a hell of a lot today. She had watched her family die, and had nearly been killed herself. She stood by as she watched her home burst into flames with everything and everyone she loved still inside. And then there was Bobby who she had just seen commit suicide using a tornado. A spell of dizziness swam through her mind and she fought to keep her vision focused and balance steady. She felt small and out of place at this moment, and decided to wait for the policeman that was close behind. But what about Bobby? She asked herself. What if he is in there, frightened and alone?

"Sarah!" Bobby screamed from somewhere inside of the house. "Sarah! Sarah! Sarah! Come to me Sarah! Help me Sarah!"

Sarah bounded across the porch and through the black hole where the front door used to hang. It was Bobby. He needed her, and she was not about to let him down.

The gray light disappeared behind her as she stepped through the doorway, and was replaced with many different shades of black. Everything seemed to change once she was inside of the house. She could no longer hear the roar of the tornado, and felt almost as if she had traveled back in time to that ancient civilization she had envisioned had occupied these imagined ruins long ago. The only illumination was the stark empty images of the windows and doorway that let in odd shadows of light. Sarah looked around in wonder and fear as she searched for Bobby.

"Bobby?" Sarah called out quietly. "Bobby, are you in here?" There was no answer, and she continued deeper into the dark room. Her eyes quickly adjusted to the darkness, and she found herself in the midst of a destroyed home. It was not the ancient ruin in which she had envisioned, but the remnants of someone's shattered life.

"Bobby?" she called again to no avail. She looked over the room thoughtfully. Everything was displaced and broken, and she carefully walked around the splintered furniture as she made her way through the darkness.

"Over here." She heard Bobby say from another part of the room, and she quickly made her way over to where she thought he might be. She moved hastily through the maze of clutter that was strewn everywhere, and her fears subsided as her expectations of seeing Bobby rose.

"I'm coming Bobby," Sarah assured. "Where are you? It is hard to see. Are you all right?" she asked, but received no reply. As she went her foot caught something solid and she lost her balance. Her stomach tightened into a knot as she went down hard onto the floor and the mess that covered it. With a flash of bright pain she screamed as her shoulder caught the leg of an overturned coffee table, and her knee struck some object that she had failed to see in the eerie non-light that filled the room. She landed awkwardly on the jumble scattered over the floor, and screamed again as she looked up and found herself facing a shoe with somebody's foot in it. She scrambled to her feet even as she was backing away from the body. Immediately she saw that it was not Bobby, but an older woman. She was not very old, possibly in her fifties. Though most adults looked old to Sarah, who was still quite young. The woman appeared to be dead, as she was lying in what looked like an extremely painful position. Her face was covered with blood, and her eyes stared sightlessly skyward. The flesh on the right side of her face had been peeled back, leaving the cheek and jawbones grotesquely visible while the long flap of skin hung loosely aside looking like a worn piece of terry cloth.

Covering her mouth Sarah held back the scream that she felt caught in her lungs. Her heart was pounding so fast and hard that she could feel it throughout her entire body. Nervously she looked around the dark room as she swallowed hard as a lump began to grow in her throat and fresh tears swelled behind her eyes.

"Bobby?" she tried to say, though it came out in a gargled whisper. Clearing her throat, she tried again. "Bobby? Bobby where are you?" she said clearly as the tears pushed past her eyes and rolled down her pale cheeks. Once again there was no answer, though she thought that she heard the body of the woman move as something underneath her shifted or gave way. Or perhaps she is alive, Sarah thought suddenly. Maybe this poor woman was alive and needed help? What if it had been this woman that she had heard calling? Maybe this lady's daughter was named Sarah as well. Sarah didn't know. She studied the grossly disfigured body of the woman, trying to see if she was breathing, though she could not tell. The woman looked dead, and Sarah kicked the lady's shoe. Still there was nothing. Turning away Sarah saw movement out of the corner of her eye. The old woman's shoulder and eye had twitched, she was almost certain of it. Turning back to the woman she once again looked and waited though saw nothing. With a shaking hand Sarah reached out and quickly poked the lady, and again there was nothing, so as terrified as she was she decided to check for a pulse. She had seen this done on television countless times, and knew how to check her own pulse. She was afraid to touch the old woman, but slowly reached in anyway, determined to find out if she was alive. With her hands shaking worse than ever she stretched out her arm and took hold of the woman's wrist.

The bloody old woman's eyes snapped open as she let out a gargled laugh, and before Sarah had a chance to withdraw her hand the woman had taken a hold of her trembling wrist, grabbing it painfully, and pulled her close. Sarah's throat let out the scream that she had been holding in as she struggled against the dead woman's grasp.

"Sarah! Sarah! Sarah! Sarah! Sarah!" the old woman screamed somehow using Bobby's voice.

"No!" Sarah cried, as she began shaking her head while trying to pull free. "NO!" she yelled again, and then continued screaming.

155

The old woman's face twisted as she spoke again, though this time it was not Bobby's voice, nor was it the voice of a lady. It was a voice that was familiar to Sarah, and terrified her as much as any monster could.

"Come here Sarah! Come give daddy a kiss!" the vile woman hissed with an evil grin as she continued pulling Sarah towards her. The remnants of her bloodied lips were pursed and ready to receive as her chest heaved with anticipation.

"No!" Sarah screamed again, and did not stop as she struggled in vain against the horrible woman. Tears fled from her wide eyes as she tried everything that was within her power to get away, but it was not enough. She reached back with her free arm, searching for something to hold onto, but found nothing stable enough to give her any leverage. Though her hand settled on a long piece of wood just as the police officer ran through the door.

"Hey! Where are you?" Jack yelled as he gazed across the dark room, quickly finding Sarah. She was screaming, crying, and in trouble.

Sarah did not wait to be rescued, and gripped the long wooden pole, that might have once been the leg of a table or chair. Summoning up all of the strength she could muster she swung the make shift club at the woman's head. Sarah's club struck the woman with an audible crack, and she thought that she could hear the woman's skull bones fracture. The blow landed squarely on the woman's temple, and her head rocked back and forth, reminding Sarah of one of those bobble headed dolls. She had swung the club so hard that it was jarred from her hand as it struck, landing deep in the dark shadowed recesses of the room. It was a good hit, though the woman did not let go. Sarah did feel the woman's grip loosen momentarily. Bringing up her legs, Sarah pushed against the lady with her feet, and all of her might, and within a few seconds she pulled herself free. Scrambling backwards as fast as she could Sarah bumped into Jack and screamed again.

"It's okay now!" Jack told her as he helped her to her feet. "Are you all right? Can you walk?"

Sarah nodded yes with a dazed look in her eyes as they turned towards the door. The woman no longer moved or talked, looking just as dead as she had when Sarah had first seen her. She wanted to get out of here, to get away as fast as she could, but as they turned to leave she saw the shadow people. They were here.

Jack put his arm around the child and began leading her through the maze of rubble that surrounded them. She was shaken and terrified. He did not know what had happened, or why she had struck the dead lady, but just wanted to get her out of here, out of danger to someplace safe. He then saw something out of the corner of his eye that made him flinch. It was a shadow. A shadow of what, he did not know. Though as he held onto Sarah

157

and prepared to run the sentinels appeared, and came at them by the hundreds.

13

Erin followed after Jack as quickly as she could, but was several minutes behind him and struggling to catch up. Her deepest fears were realized when she saw him standing in front of the tornado alone, the children no where in sight. She then saw him dash into the old brick house, and her hopes were resurrected. The tornado was a wicked looking sight in front of her, and she tried to ignore the uneasy feelings that surfaced in her mind, intent on concentrating on what she could and would do when she found the children, though she feared that she may be too late. All she wanted to do was get the children to some place safe, and she had decided that she would get them to this safe place if she had to knock them out to do it. Though mostly she just prayed that they were all right.

As she neared the old house Erin felt as if she had exhausted every ounce of strength she had. She slowed her pace as she grew closer broken old home. She hoped that the kids had taken refuge inside the old house, and that the tornado would move away. She didn't think that she could handle another brush with death with her sanity still intact. She felt as if she were already over the edge, and hanging on by her belt loop. It had completely stopped raining by the time she reached the old house, and she was filled with hope and fear as she neared the front porch. Brushing her fear aside she jumped up onto the small deck even as she heard the sounds of struggle coming from beyond the doorway.

"Get them off me! Get them off me!" she heard Jack shouting frantically. It was incredibly dark inside of the house, and she stopped at the entranceway to see what she was walking into. She could hear Sarah crying and whimpering, but it took a moment for her eyes to adjust to the darkness, and for her to believe what she was seeing. The room itself seemed to be alive as shadow melted with shadow, and it was then that she realized that it was the shadow people in which she was looking at. The sentinels were here, and were attacking Jack and Sarah in what she could only describe as vengeful glee. She didn't know what to do, though as the adrenalin fled through her she acted on instinct, right or wrong. Bobby had not been afraid of the shadow people, but he was special, and she did not see him here, and her heart froze at the thought of what had become of him. She burst into the room and grabbed up Sarah's arm, intending to pull her out of there, but was stopped dead in her tracks when she turned to leave.

The sentinel was everywhere. There were hundreds if not thousands of them. The sentinel was like a force of nature as they all moved and worked together as one. It was an all consuming mass of darkness that converged upon her, trying to get into her, trying to possess her. Screaming unaware, she tried to get away, but as she looked back to where the door had been she found nothing but darkness, and it was then that she realized that she could not see anything. Disoriented and confused she took a step forward to where she thought the door had been, but tripped over something that was lying on the ground and crashed down hard onto floor and into the clutter. As she fell she let go of Sarah's arm, and when she turned around she could no longer see the child, and even her screams seemed muted and far away.

It was like a feeding frenzy, and Erin and the others were the food. The Sentinel swam through them as if they were made of air. It was a suffocating feeling, and Erin could feel the grasp of death as they overcame her. It was then that she thought she understood the Sentinel, she believed them to be the force that consumed the souls of the dead, the thieves of life. She didn't know if they were good or bad, or neither, or perhaps this was god's way of collecting the souls of the deceased to be released elsewhere. In any case, she could feel them trying to steal her away into the void that now surrounded her. Her breaths grew shorter and more labored and it felt to her as if her asthma was returning ten-fold.

Tears escaped Erin's tired eyes as she fought to sustain her grip on reality and the life she feared was draining away. Her heart was saddened to have survived so much this day, only to perish in a wave of supernatural chaos. Life was cruel.

Then, almost as if they had never been there, the sentinel was gone. Erin's eyesight returned and she caught a brief glimpse of them as their sleek, shadowy forms disappeared through the cracks in the walls, floor, and ceiling. She saw Sarah and Jack as they sat up looking horrified, but healthy, and she went to them.

"Are you guy's all right? Where is Bobby?" Erin asked fearfully.

Sarah and Jack looked to each other sadly, and then back to Erin.

Jack shook his head solemnly. "I am sorry," he said.

"No!" Erin said as fresh tears leaked from her eyes. "Where is he? I want to see him."

"He went into the tornado," Sarah said as she looked down to the floor.

Getting to her feet Erin slowly walked to the door. She unsuccessfully choked back the feelings and emotions that were running through her like a flood, and she decided that she could take no more, and was ready to give in to the will of the tornado.

Though as she looked outside she saw that the twister was losing strength, and appeared to be dying out. She watched as the shadow creatures slipped from shadow to shadow towards and into the twister, and then they were gone completely. Bowing her head she wiped away the tears as she thought of the unique little boy that she had failed to save.

"It is breaking," Erin said through the lump that was steadily growing in the back of her throat. "I think it is almost over."

Jack and Sarah helped each other to their feet, and followed Erin as she walked out of the broken old house. The tornado was dissipating, and as it's strength decreased the debris it carried began to rain down everywhere. They stood there silently watching as the twister weakened until it was just an immense swirl of dust on the ground. There was destruction everywhere. Nothing within sight had been left untouched by the tornado, and even the land bore it's terrible scorch mark. The clouds to the south began to break apart as they moved towards them and brilliant shards of sunlight shown down onto the distant landscape. They shot down like tremendous spotlights out of the heavens, and Erin's attention was drawn to the lovely display.

"It is beautiful!" Sarah exclaimed as she walked off of the porch to get a better view.

It was beautiful, though Erin could not keep her eyes from the swirling remnants of the tornado, and her mind from the strange little boy in which she had grown to love in the short time they had been together. It was strange, she thought, how such a horrible thing as the tornado could be a part of the same storm to yield such a wondrous sight as the radiant beams of white light shining down like obscure shadows of light. The light caught the drizzle from the clouds around them and made rainbows to the like she had never seen before. The unstable storm front caused the winds to shift continuously, and it made the colors move as if they were alive and flowing. It was beautiful, possibly one of the most beautiful things she had ever seen, but she would not let herself enjoy it at Bobby's expense.

"Oh my god!" Jack shrieked as he ran ahead of them. "Did you see that?" he asked eagerly.

"See what?" Erin asked as she noticed that he was pointing to the dusty cloud where the tornado had vanished.

"I can see it!" Sarah exclaimed, as she too looked deeper into the smoky remains of the twister.

"See what?" Erin asked again as she too looked deeper into the haze, and then saw what might have been the shadowy outline of people, though she could not be certain, and her thoughts drifted to the Sentinel, and she grew apprehensive.

"I do see something," Erin admitted as she stepped closer.

"It is him!" Sarah screamed, and then began running towards the haze.

"What is going on here?" Jack asked. "And what were those things in there?" he demanded to know as he pointed back to the old brick house from which they had just escaped.

"Just a minute," Erin said, trying her best not to ignore him as she saw movement in the dust. There were three shadowy forms emerging from the haze, and one of them was the slight figure of a child. "Bobby?" she called out, though she didn't really expect an answer if it was him, and she did not receive one. New tears of hope trickled down her cheeks as she ran with Sarah towards the strangers.

Jack couldn't believe his eyes, even as he watched the small child emerge from the remnants of the tornado, and he followed immediately behind Erin. It is impossible! Jack told himself, for anyone to have survived such a horrendous twister, though here was the boy, and he was not alone. As they grew closer Jack could see that the boy had an elderly couple with him, and appeared to be leading them out of the debris. Bobby was in the middle of the two strangers, and each of them held one of his hands. Jack almost didn't believe what he was seeing, but could not deny the truth that was in front of him, and the word miracle kept popping into his mind.

Sarah was the first to reach Bobby and the older couple. She had tears streaming down her face, and almost knocked Bobby down when she embraced him.

"I thought you were dead!" Sarah cried, as Bobby released the stranger's hands and hugged her tightly.

Erin had no idea how Bobby had managed to stay alive through the tornado, while saving two more people in the process. In truth, she did not care. All that she knew at this moment was that she was overjoyed to see him again, and could not help laughing through her tears.

"Is everybody all right?" Erin asked as she and Jack reached Bobby, Sarah, and the elderly couple. Bobby nodded, and Sarah said nothing as she clung to Bobby as if her life depended on it.

Erin then looked up to the elderly couple. They looked as haggard and worn as the rest of them, but did not appear to be injured. "How about you two? Are you okay?" she asked them.

The old woman nodded and then looked over to her husband. "Yes I think so. Are you all right Cliff?"

The aged gentleman shook his head with a smile. "I feel as good as new," he said. "That was one hell of a storm!"

"Oh Cliff, you and your storms," the old lady laughed. "You may be okay physically, but I think that you should have your head examined."

"Now Ruby, be nice," Cliff jested.

"I am sorry," Ruby said with a weathered smile. "Where are my manners? I am Ruby Meadows, and this is my husband Cliff. And well, you already know Robert," she said as she ruffled

Bobby's wet hair. "Welcome to our home," she said as she looked to the devastation that surrounded them.

"My name is Erin, and this is Jack and Sarah," said Ruby as she shook Ruby's hand and then Cliff's. "And it appears that you already know Bobby here, who we have been chasing for the better part of the afternoon."

"That's my Bobby," Ruby said as Sarah finally let the boy go, and he quickly went to Ruby's side and hugged her around the waist.

"So you know him?" Erin asked.

Ruby nodded with a smile. "It has been some time, but now it feels as if he never left us," she said as she gave Bobby a tight squeeze around the shoulders, and a kiss on top of his head.

"Left us?" Erin questioned.

"Fifty years ago yesterday," Cliff said proudly as he patted Bobby on the head.

"What do you mean?" Erin asked with a puzzled expression and wonder in her eyes.

"Oh my god!" Jack interrupted. "Would you look at that? Have you ever seen anything like it?" he asked everyone as he pointed towards the brilliant shards of sunlight that shown down out of the heavens.

The clouds were flowing overhead with a quickness like Erin had never before seen, and it reminded her of the time-lapse photography that allowed her to watch flowers grow and bloom within seconds on television. It was incredible, though her eyes were drawn to a white piece of paper that lay at her feet.

"Wow!" Sarah said as she took up Erin's hand into her own. "Look Erin! It is beautiful!"

"It sure is honey," said Erin as she held Sarah's hand with her left, and picked up the light white square with her right. As she turned it over she saw that it was a photograph. On closer inspection she noticed that it was a picture of Bobby and his parents. The photo looked old and worn, and had been taken in black and white. As she studied the photo she realized that Bobby's parents could only be Ruby and Cliff, as the resemblance was unmistakable. She began to grow lightheaded and dizzy when she finally understood what this meant. Trying to come to terms with what was happening she looked up to the heavens and watched as the stunning rays of sunlight moved closer to them. They were coming fast, and she tracked the shadows of light as they moved quickly across the landscape. Within a moment the rays of light had reached them, and Erin felt her stomach begin to flutter and turn as the light struck her, giving her the strangest sensation of being weightless. She watched as the photograph appeared to lose its substance. Becoming transparent it slipped through her fingers and fell slowly towards the ground. Looking up she saw nothing but the warm light that seemed to carry her away

14

Running as fast as he could, Todd sidestepped and leapt over the debris strewn throughout the yard as he made his way towards the school. The storm seemed to be breaking as the rain and thunder had stopped, and the strong winds had diminished to a faint breeze. There were even odd peeks of sunlight in the distance that seemed out of place amidst the destruction that nature had unleashed. Though he took little or no notice of anything as he made his way out of Brad's yard. His mind was enveloped with thoughts and worries for Erin, and he fought against the unbridled emotion that threatened to bring him to tears.

"Damn it!" Todd shouted as his exposed foot found another piercing nail, though he did not stop or even slow down, but instead pushed himself faster and more recklessly.

He could see dense curls of black smoke coming from behind the school where he and Brad had heard the explosion. Flames shot up towards the sky, and from where he was it looked as if the school was burning as well.

People were beginning to come out of their houses. The ones who had been lucky enough not to have been in the twister's path stared at the devastation with wild-eyed wonder. There was screaming everywhere, and Todd tried not to hear them, as he feared that one of the painful wails might be Erin's.

He raced out into the street and towards the school. He wasn't that far away, but time seemed to slow down as he ran, and it seemed to be taking a long time to go such a short distance. His mind was spinning, as his thought swam in and out of focus, and consisted of all of the possibilities that time had to offer, of all past, present, and future. He thought about his life here in Northern Illinois, and of what it could have been someplace else. He also thought about the scores of people who he had helped and saved since becoming an Emergency Medical Technician. He knew that Harvard was much different when compared to the bigger cities, as he had heard Erin talk of the differences and the similarities over the past year. Here, nine out of ten times you knew the person who was in trouble, or at least knew somebody who did. You would see them again driving down the street or in the grocery store, and it gave Todd a warm sense of fulfillment to be able to see and meet the people who's lives he had touched.

He thought of his music, and of his dreams that seemed to be getting harder to grasp with each passing year. He would have given them all up for Erin, if she had asked, and he now prayed that she would live to have that argument with him. He knew that she would have never asked such a thing from him. She was open minded and honest, and had a lust for life that equaled his own. She was special in ways that he could not rightly explain, and was unlike anyone he had ever met.

He remembered the first time they had met, and the strange look of suspicion and interest she had shown upon seeing his long dark hair. He thought that he had known what she was thinking at that moment. Oh no, I have to work with a hippie! He had imagined her thinking that he was some longhaired freak that probably worked to support his drug habit. Though she had not responded in that way at all, and had instead commented on how much she would love to have such beautiful hair. Yes, she was special.

Reaching the school he gasped as he saw the horrific sight of the mangled ambulance that had been thrown most of the way through the school wall. His stomach dropped out from inside of him as he ran to the ambulance in terror. Never before had he seen such a horrible sight, and the emotion that he had been fighting against broke free as tears began to stream out of his watery eyes. Listening to the screams and cries for help as he went, he now hoped that Erin's voice was a part of that eerie chorus, as it would mean that she was still alive. He knew that her chances were slim to nil, though he held onto a slight bit of hope that helped carry him through.

"If anyone is strong enough to make it through this, Erin would be the one!" he told himself as he raced across the school's deserted parking lot. "She would not let me down, not Erin!" he assured himself skeptically.

Weary and out of breath Todd reached the ambulance, which was leaning awkwardly on its side. The driver's compartment was the only part of the vehicle not to have gone through the wall of the school, and stuck out from the brick wall like the head of a dead dinosaur. The windshield had been shattered, and the broken glass added to the searing pain in his shoeless foot as he slid to a stop.

"Erin! Erin?" he screamed as he frantically peered through the gaping hole where the windshield had once been, and then looked away pensively as fresh tears rolled down his quivering chin. There was blood everywhere, and he knew that he had been too late, that her death had happened quickly, probably even before the tornado had reached her. He fought against his horror and looked back to where Erin's bloodied corpse lay. Her expression frozen in a state of shock, as her sightless eyes stared forward into oblivion.

"**No! No! No!**" Todd screamed over and over again as his tears kept falling. He found his hands shaking badly as he reached through the fractured windshield, and ran his fingers through her beautiful blood stained auburn hair. Closing his eyes, Todd prayed that this might be a dream, and that when he opened his eyes again he would find himself at home, or in the ambulance snoozing as he waited for a call. But this did not happen. Erin was dead, either by the crash or the tornado. It didn't matter how it had happened, she was dead and he was unable to help her. Not then, not now, and not ever, and he tried to push away the thoughts of what he had imagined their future could have been like together. He closed her dry eyes and cried as he listened the cries of the living as they called out for help.

Turning away from Erin he sat down and rested his back against the ambulance. He knew that Erin would not be the only fatality in the catastrophe, and that there would be many others that he could save. Trying once again to hold back his emotions he stood up and went to the back of the ambulance. He gathered up all of the bandages and other necessary tools he could find or salvage and walked away, leaving Erin behind. Limping away from the school and out of the parking lot he cried as a plethora of injured and needy people awaited his attention.

Three days later

After finishing packing his van with all of his belongings Todd looked around to the beautiful day that surrounded him. He had just left the memorial service held in Erin's honor, and was preparing to leave for Arizona, where Erin's body was to be sent, and the funeral ultimately held. Feeling numb, he climbed into the driver's seat and started the engine. There was so much that he was leaving behind, a lifetime of memories, both good and bad. He had dreamed up leaving this place for as long as he could remember, but he had never imagined that it would be under these circumstances, and for the moment at least, it did nothing to ease his pain and sense of loss.

He put the old van in gear and left his old life behind in search of a new one. He would find the challenge that he had been looking for, though first he would attend Erin's funeral, and tell her family of the countless people in which she had helped and inspired while living in Illinois, as Todd was one of them.

About The Author

Eric has enjoyed writing for as far back as he can remember, and has not lost his lust for words. Every second of every day is a probable novel, and each moment a potential preface. Fiction and non-fiction is all relative and subject to interpretation.

His primary years were spent in the Illinois suburbs of Chicago. At the age of nine he moved to Arizona where he grew to love the environment and culture of the region, which only enriched his joy of writing, and his love for the mysteries of life. He finished high school early and joined the Navy where he became a Hospital Corpsman, and Emergency Medical Technician. He served his county on the ambulance crew as well as in the emergency room, and on more than one occasion was chosen to serve as medical coverage for the Space Shuttle.

Eric went to college in Orlando Florida while in the Navy, and after a number of years left the service and spent many months exploring Arizona, as well as himself.

Eric now lives in southern Wisconsin with his wife and children, and although life demands more than he has, he continues to write, and after you have read Ruby Meadows, Shadows Of Light, you will know why. It is because we are all merely shadows of light, the tracer that is left on your eye after you look at the sun.

Printed in the United States
20038LVS00001B/181

9 781418 427061